Praise for *A Simple Machine, Like the Lever*

"Clever, poignant, and unexpectedly funny, Schneider's *A Simple Machine, Like The Lever* masterfully evokes the simple pleasures—and harsh realities—of keeping to one's ideals in a world where speed is revered and complexity is king."

—David Rozgonyi, author of *Goat Trees: Tales from the Other Side of the World*

"Evan P. Schneider's debut novel, *A Simple Machine, Like the Lever*, is exactly that: a deceptively simple, efficient, and potentially revolutionary machine. Like its co-protagonists—Nick and his bicycle—the novel cranks out quietly subversive, smart, and funny prose that crackles with insights on the current human condition; a book that, while never polemical, seduces you into fully re-examining the stuff of your life and somehow convinces you that the answer lies in reducing, reusing, and riding...just riding."

—Steven Church, author of *The Day After* The Day After*: My Atomic Angst*

"All the fresh pleasures of taking a bike ride are to be found in *A Simple Machine, Like the Lever*. The novel is by turns innocent, lyrical, wistful, funny, and poignant. Necessity has made its observant narrator, Nick, hopelessly thrifty, but what has made him so bafflingly sweet?"

—Mary Rechner, author of *Nine Simple Patterns for Complicated Women*

“Evan P. Schneider’s literary cycling uplift is enough to counteract the weight of the world. He nails the essence of being a cyclist and of being young—the yearning, the detachment, the attempted grace, the uncertainty, the gray confusion.”

—Jonny Waldman, founder of Zero Per Gallon ($0.00 9/10)

“Just as a simple machine is defined as ‘a mechanical device that changes the direction or magnitude of force,’ Schneider’s *A Simple Machine, Like the Lever* is a literary creation that changes the reader’s intellect and heart. With sincere and engaging narration, Schneider unfolds the spirit and the flaws, the sorrows and the loves of an endearing character whose honest observations transcend the conventional cultural obsessions with profit, convenience, and speed. Like a child lifted upon a teeter-totter, like a rider propelled upon a bicycle, the reader is carried back to the invaluable world one can never purchase, and given again the too-often forgotten splendors of everyday life.”

—Erzsébet Gilbert, author of *Logodædaly, or, Sleight-of-Words*

# A Simple Machine, Like the Lever

# A Simple Machine, Like the Lever

*a novel*

Evan P. Schneider

Published by Propeller Books, Portland, Oregon.
ISBN 978-0-9827704-1-2
First U.S. Edition 2011

Cover art and design by E.L. Swift

Parts of this book originally appeared in slightly different form in *Boneshaker: A Bicycling Almanac* and *Propeller,* as well as on *Carfree American.*

www.propellerbooks.com

Printed in Canada

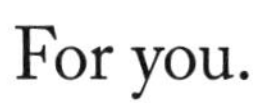
For you.

# 1

THIS MORNING, when I put on my pants, I went ahead and just rolled them up right away. I rolled them up so that I could save time later when I'm out in the yard, packing up my lock, putting on my bag, putting on my helmet, and getting ready to go.

Despite my routine, it never fails that I forget something, one thing every morning, and it's usually rolling up my pants. Half a block into my commute it will surprise me. I will be looking up to see what the clouds are doing for the day and if I was right to wear only a long-sleeved shirt and my light brown sweater, the one I wear most often, with the little hole in the right elbow.

Then I'll think, *Gloves?* Yes, got them. *Polypropylene undersocks?* Check. I always wear two pairs of socks: undersocks to wick moisture and an outer pair for warmth and comfort. The under layer is white and the outer layer is argyle.

If I don't roll up my pants, within half a block my pant leg will get spit out the underside of the chain ring. Then my pants will have little greasy teeth marks on them from being creased in the cogs. That's not so bad, but oil never really washes out of the pant leg, even if I soak the thing for hours and then scrub it with one of those fancy scrubber liquids they sell with the brush built right into the top of the dispenser. Greasy marks on pants may very well ruin them forever. When that happens, and the pant leg gets pulled through the bike's fine inner workings, not only have I potentially disfigured my pants, but I still have to stop and get off and roll them up.

But that's not what makes me mad. What makes me mad is the thought that I am going to rip the only pair of decent pants I own, which I have to have for work. Pants are expensive, and they don't fit into the matrix of month-to-month spending I devised for myself after I ran out of money and available credit and resources about this time three years ago. Nowadays I can buy a new pair of pants once every seven months and still be all right. But that's only if I don't rip them somewhere in their allotted lifespan. Good new professional pants, ones that Greg won't have a problem with me wearing into the office, run somewhere between $75 and $100. In this equation one pair of pants equals about three different dates with Marie, if we keep to happy hour, or one fancier time together, which

I'll admit I'm not able to do too often. One pair of new work pants also equals out to around the cost of some new pedals, which I could really use, or about 0.2% of the total debt I've been working at paying off to feel okay again.

This is why I rolled up my pants this morning when I put them on: because I decided it was time to make a change. To eliminate the possibility of forgetting to roll up my pants during "crunch time," as I call that hectic span of minutes just before I'm leaving, I did it when I put them on in the first place. This means that for the whole hour and a half before I left the house, I walked around with my pants folded up, argyle socks visible to the cats at eye level.

Air comes in at your legs when you have your pants rolled even just that much. It creeps up to where the top of your sock ends and where your pants don't ever touch your skin. Below the fatness of your knee the material of pants orbits your leg and normally keeps it warm out of proximity. But when your pants are rolled up, air gets up in there and is able to rub against your flesh and draw attention back to the fact that you have your work pants rolled up indoors at home because you only own one pair.

Then I caught myself in the mirror. It looked as if I was getting ready for a long afternoon of digging in hard soil, when in fact I was just going to ride a bicycle across the city to a business that sells sinks. But if this rolling technique keeps my pants from getting ripped, I suppose I'll try it again tomorrow. That will be positive progress.

I just don't want to be thought of as one of those people

who wears his pants rolled up constantly, though, because I'm not.

# 2

---

THE SMELLS through which I get to pedal on my way to work are really something. Today I experienced these:

+ fireplace smoke

+ train yard smell

+ coffee, which I could tell was being roasted

+ the scent of dryer sheets billowing from the vents on the side of an apartment complex

I never tire of different smells. This morning, I found myself thinking of the way the world comes at me through my nose. What I smelled most was moist grass, a smell that is actually one of the strongest you can happen upon when you're zipping through the air at a clip, a smell that has a way of crowding out other, less dominant scents. I thought about the fact that I smelled both fireplace smoke and cut grass in the same day, and that one could defeat the other in the echelons of olfactory sensation.

Truck exhaust is a terrible, suffocating smell.

I've never understood smell, just like I've never understood wind. How smell can permeate a shower experience, for example, I don't know. Scents don't get wet, apparently, which is a disturbing and miraculous fact that makes me glad I'm not a scientist. I've even tried wetting a smell. In the shower, if I happen to pass gas—which I try not to make a habit of doing because I've showered with Marie a number of times and I don't want to have an unacceptable habit that I'll do unconsciously in her presence—I'll step out of the way and aim the pulsing stream of water down toward where the smell is invisibly emanating from, and yet: nothing. The vague stale scent will not be quelled.

Sometimes when I get home from work I'll take off my shirt and put it on the chair. Then I'll think, *What's that smell?* I buy most of my shirts at Goodwill, so I often figure it must be someone else's scent still embedded in the threads. But no. If I smell under my arm, that oniony smell is always me.

# 3

---

Today a man in a rickety truck drove behind me for a few hundred feet and honked. I'm not sure what he was trying to communicate. "Careful, right behind you!" or "Hey, asshole!" or "What are you doing there on that bike in the road? How does it feel?" The horn is such a poor communicator because it can mean so many things.

In general, I focus intently on what people are saying, but all I can think is, *That's not the word you mean. What you mean is this other word. The way you are saying it really goes against the point you are trying to make.* So then, instead of absorbing what someone is trying to say, I dwell on what they're *actually* telling me, which is very different in a lot of cases from what they want to communicate.

The other day, for example, I pulled up to Marie's on my bike. Her house is small and has a symmetrical two-tone color combination, beige on the bottom and dark red on top. It's very cozy.

"I think your fender's coming off," she said, eating an apple as I rode up. Marie is petite and slender, as though she never indulges in too much of anything that's not good for her. She has a vintage and respectable 1980's Heather Locklear look to her, but I've never said that because I don't know if everyone likes Heather Locklear as much as I do.

But my fender wasn't coming off, because I don't have fenders, so I said, "You mean my reflector?"

"Just take it easy, Shakespeare," she said. "You know what I mean. The part on your handlebar that's dangling."

The man in the truck made it clearer what he meant, however, by honking and extending the middle finger of his right hand while he passed me. His baseball cap was dirty and pulled down low. His beard was much fuller than mine and creeped down into his shirt. Then he really put his foot into the accelerator and made distance between us.

*Surely that was uncalled-for,* I thought.

I rode calmly for a few seconds, just watching my legs pump up and down in the morning light, but then my heart started to beat faster and I could taste something acidic in my mouth. I sped up. He would be at the stoplight, I was sure of it, because it's a very long light in that direction, so I rode swiftly around three corners and cut through a parking lot to catch him.

At the intersection, though, he wasn't there. He must have made the green. I was at the long red. *Probably for the best*, I thought. What was I going to do, anyway? Say, "Excuse me, there. You passed me a while back and honked. What did you mean by that, exactly?"

Of course I wouldn't say that. I would probably just pull up and look at him through the passenger side window for a long time and not say anything, just staring at him sitting there.

Then the light turned green.

The rest of the ride, I thought about his finger. I also thought about the face he was making, contorted in fury as he glanced at me. How that one finger can destroy my spirit so easily is disheartening.

The clouds were thick and the morning quiet, so I tried to think of something else.

When I was about eleven, I would ride from my family's house on a dusty country road several miles into town to buy a candy bar at Suzie's Market. A Big Hunk. After that I would play some hoops in a friend's driveway or walk along the railroad tracks and hide in the trees when the train came. I liked the fact that the train didn't know I was there, watching it go by. I couldn't believe how such a large machine could move so smoothly. Then I'd ride home again before dark.

No one ever honked at me then. Even really large trucks filled with sugarbeets gave me a wide berth.

The finger the man in the truck waved in my direction

was, in a way, like those giant foam fingers at baseball games that my dad took me to once or twice around that same age when I was hiding from trains. I remembered being enthralled with the fact that you could buy at the stadium and wear on your hand another hand that was enormously exaggerated and that proclaimed your team was #1. It wasn't merely the hugeness of the finger that entertained me, which it did, but that two fans, rooting for two different teams playing in the same game, could simultaneously be wearing a foam finger in the same stadium, each of which said "#1."

Usually, before we would even get into the stadium, I remembered, some man would be yelling, "Got tickets here! Cheap tickets!" Then a few steps closer to the turnstile a different man would be holding up a piece of cardboard on which was written, "I need tickets!" As we walked by, he would say, "Extra tickets?"

So once I said, "That guy has some. He's selling tickets right there." Then I pointed to the man we just passed who said he had tickets. But my dad said we should keep walking because that's not what the men meant.

I was gliding now, my heart rate back to normal. *Everyone has places to be*, I thought. *We're all number one.*

# 4

---

My new morning experiment worked.

I didn't forget to roll up my pants. Indeed, how could I, seeing as how I had already taken care of it when I put them on? And so my ride to work was undemanding.

I even had a minute to talk to the homeless man on the corner. He's always there, sitting cross-legged on the sidewalk with a group of toy dinosaurs surrounding him. There's also a small cardboard sign that says something different everyday. He is the nicest man.

"Beautiful smile," he'll say if he happens to notice you pass, which he sometimes doesn't. Sometimes he's sort of sleeping when I ride by, head hanging in his lap. His neck probably hurts quite often, and there's a stain on the sidewalk where he sits.

Today, taking advantage of the stop sign and following

the law by putting my foot down for a few seconds, I asked him how it was going.

"Oh," he said, "you know. Just waking up, going to work." Then he held up a newspaper that was covering his lap and pretended to scan it with a scrunched brow. A small bowl was positioned in front of him, but there was no loose change in it that I could see.

"Is that the TV schedule there?" I asked. "What's on tonight?"

"Oh, I don't have a TV," he said.

I have a feeling the world would like nothing more than to consume or crush him and me.

I made it to work without any teeth marks on my pants and with five minutes to spare, which I liked, because I need those five minutes, maybe more, to lock up properly. There are only a few things about cycling I don't care for, and one is the locking up and unlocking and then relocking, but wait, no, here I go unlocking again. My locking routine is very involved, with several steps to ensure my bike's utmost safety when I leave it alone in public view.

At the bike rack, one of my coworkers, Michelle, passed me. She was wearing a floral dress like usual, belted around her large waist. Michelle likes to make conversation in a loud voice with everyone she sees. She also uses your name when she talks to you.

"That's quite the system you've got there, huh, Nick?"

I was putting the cable first between the rungs of my

saddle, then through the frame, then through the back wheel, then back through the frame before going through the front wheel and finishing it off by sliding my U-lock around both ends of the cable, which I also ran up between the two uppermost holes in my helmet (I leave my helmet with my bike) to create a secure circuitous loop. I brought the lock closed, effectively clamping wheel and frame in a tidy, intimidating web. "Can't be too safe," I said, because it's true. You can't.

If someone really wanted to, though, they could just bring a pair of heavy-duty cable cutters and snip my whole set-up in a flash. Or they could smuggle a hacksaw up to my bike and go at the lock that way.

I've noticed that if you seem to know what you're doing, or at least exude confidence that your actions are sanctioned, like a city worker on a ladder, you can really do anything you want. This is how I fear my bike will be stolen, despite the fortress I erect around it each day. Someone with a conspicuous, efficient scythe will approach my bike in broad daylight and act as if he or she's supposed to be doing so, cutting the bike away, and zero cries of protest will rise up from passersby.

Michelle watched as I finished my routine. "Seems like it takes a lot of time and energy," she said.

Then I said something really stupid. I said, "That's the price you pay for being free." I don't know what that had to do with locking up my bike.

Michelle is having a bad day every day I've ever talked to her. She asks questions like, "Hey, Nick, have you ever had to describe your working philosophy?" but before I can answer she says, still in the same fast breath, "because Greg has asked me to explain my work philosophy in one page. Can you believe that?" Yes, in fact, I can believe that very easily. Greg is our boss and makes demands of our time when we're in the office. It's very simple.

I don't know why, but people often want to give me too much information in conversation, information I haven't asked for but that they want to share regardless of my not knowing them that well or at all. Bank tellers and waiters do this, for example, tell me things that I should not know about their lives, like the fact that their spouse's colon recently collapsed. I think of these conversations as large forests I deliberately avoid by going around their perimeters, because I don't have a map or any idea how many acres their darkness spans.

One time a woman with whom I had a class in college said out loud, right after we had been let out, "God, I hate this class. All of these assignments are so dumb."

So I said, "Maybe you should drop out."

Everyone in the quasi-circle that we used to gather into after class looked at their feet.

"What?! No! I *love* college. I want to be a professor."

"It sounds like you don't like college very much at all," I said. "It sounds like you hate it."

No one in that class hung out with me much after that, so I sort of regretted saying it, even though it was true.

I don't think Michelle really wanted to know about locking up a bicycle. She just wanted *to ask* about locking up a bicycle. And after my really stupid comment about being free, she just said, "Oh. All right." Then she walked the rest of the way to the office and left me by myself.

# 5

---

Here are a few things I saw today on my ride home from work:

+ wind chimes, which didn't chime until I rode by

+ a man with one leg pedaling a bicycle uphill

+ someone taking a lick off of another person's ice cream cone

+ a dime in the road that I stopped and picked up

+ a small girl riding a large bicycle, going the wrong direction

Sometimes when I ride I can't keep from policing other riders in my mind. I pay close attention to the way everyone else rides their bicycles, because I want to ride my own in the calmest, most beautiful way possible. My goal is to expend only the minimum necessary energy, and to let the bicycle do its elegant work beneath me. The bicycle has been called man's noblest invention (though the microscope is also pretty impressive), and when people see me ride by, as they sit in a steel chair at a patio café or as they look out the windows of the bank where they are making a deposit, I hope they'll see me and think, *That man there is having a very easy time of life and transportation.*

That's what I'm striving for, but some roads are very long. By watching others I hope to pick up pointers. Many bicyclists are far better than I am at riding, and look as if they're not even moving their bodies while they glide above the street tops, as if city planners have finally installed those $22^{nd}$-century walkways that take us everywhere, and all we have to do is stand in place and get whisked about. Often, though, I get angry at how people ride, like the girl going in the wrong direction this afternoon. Marie says I should just choose not to care, but I don't see how that's possible.

After I got home and was already sweaty, I exercised in my apartment. It's a short regimen I came up with that I complete some afternoons in private. I don't have any weights or one of those nifty all-in-one super infomercial machines that works every one of my 237 individual muscle groups. I just do sit-ups and pushups and use my desk chair as a curl bar.

Here's what my routine looks like:

+ 3 sets of 50 crunches

+ 3 sets of 25 pushups

+ 3 sets of 20 chair curls

Then, I do:

+ 1 set of 55 side crunches, on each side

+ 1 set of 35 pushups

+ 1 set of 25 chair curls

At the end, I finish with:

+ 1 set of 125 leg raises

+ 1 set of 50 pushups (which I sometimes have to break into 2 sets of 25)

+ 1 set of 35 chair curls

I guess I should also tell you that it's not uncommon for me to drink a can of beer while I exercise, which I recognize might defeat the purpose, but it's really quite relaxing.

Marie says she likes my body. I think I'm kind of squatty, so I try to keep myself as svelte as possible, because I'm not very tall. I'm convinced that if Marie breaks up with me it will be because I'm not attractive enough. Marie is stunning, and people in a relationship should match each other like the analogous slants of a parallelogram—symmetry is far more important than most people realize. I'm just average looking, so I at least try to stay toned.

If Marie does break it off with me, it might also be because I'm not much fun at night. Or because I'm thirty-one and without a career or any disposable income.

# 6

---

During my lunch break this afternoon, the man at the bookstore told me that he was not interested in my copy of D.H. Lawrence's *The Lost Girl*. "I'll pass on this one," he said.

"Okay," I said. "Thanks, anyway."

This particular man routinely scowls at me when I take books into the store hoping they'll buy them from me. Without talking, he passes back a lot of the titles I put on the counter, even though when I return on a different day and he's not working, there are other employees who will buy them from me without much consideration.

I only take in one book at a time so as not to overwhelm anybody or be much of a bother to deal with, but his coldness toward me still seems pretty clear. Maybe he has figured out that I am selling my books to pay my bills and doesn't approve of that. Or maybe he sees people like me all the time, people who are trying to whittle down their possessions because they really had no business buying them in the first place. Maybe he realizes that if he takes all of our books, each will be worth less. It's a supply and demand scenario. Things aren't ever really worth the price you pay for them. Price is only a reflection of one's willingness to own something. That's what my dad used to say, anyway. It's basic economics, I think, but it might also be philosophy.

I read three quarters of *The Lost Girl* but never finished it. I got all the way to the part where the girl marries the performer and moves to Italy. I know that's where I stopped reading because that's the point in my book where there are no more pencil marks under sentences I liked. Plus, I remember thinking that following an attractive foreigner across the continent for love was a foolish thing for that girl to do.

But there are some nice D.H. Lawrence poems that I *have* read all the way through and really enjoy, like the one that goes, "It is only immoral / to be dead-alive, / sun extinct / and busy putting out the sun / in other people." I like that.

It felt weird owning *The Lost Girl* and having it sit there on my shelf for so long when I hadn't finished it and didn't think I ever would, so I decided to sell it. The man at the bookstore passed on it, but tomorrow, if he's not working,

I bet someone else will give me two dollars for it and then another person can finish it instead. Then there will be one less thing in my life I haven't done.

# 7

---

There is a light on my bike that I stole from Marie's friend's garage.

We go over there sometimes. I don't care much for Marie's friend or her husband, but I go because that's what people do. People go to other people's houses to eat food and talk about themselves for a few hours and then hug each other and return home, where they talk about what the other people do or do not do and why.

The last several times we ventured over to Christina and Abraham's, we ended up going out into the garage during our visit for one reason or another:

+ to look at a cute new antique Christina wanted to show Marie that she was restoring

+ so that Abraham could ask me a question about a rattling noise he'd heard coming from the pipes behind the hot water heater

+ to play ping pong at the ping pong table they bought their kids for Christmas

When we were out there those times, I saw this bike light off in a corner, by a pile of odds and ends. I notice things like this everywhere. I have a collection of pennies and nickels and dimes I've found on the ground. I'm saving them to take into the bank's change counter machine. There's quite a bit of money to be made picking it up off the ground, if you just look for it. I'm hoping there's $70 or $80 worth of change in my old grape juice bottle, because then I can get some really nice pedals instead of only middle-of-the-line replacements. My pedals have really begun to make a lot of noise recently, and other riders have started to watch me as I pedal by. They probably think I don't know what I'm doing, or how to ride a bicycle properly, or what that sound is, which is exactly the opposite of what I want them to think. The fact that I have to save up for such a purchase makes it seem that I don't know what I'm doing, but I do. I just want to do things right or not at all.

In this case, though, I have to ride anyway, even if it's not the way I would really do it if I had money.

So I knew the bike light had been there in Abraham's garage for quite a while. It looked perfectly functional. But instead of being used on a bike, it was on the floor of a messy garage.

I am a firm believer in what they say: if you lose one sense, like vision, your other senses sharpen to make up for it. You start to hear quite well, or can smell as acutely as a wolverine. Not having much money makes it easy to see when it's being wasted.

Earlier today in the office, for example, there was some leftover food from the staff meeting. I know from experience and careful observation that those multigrain rolls and peanut butter would have sat on the counter for a few days until they went bad. So before anyone could come along and assume no one else in the office wanted any of it and just throw it all out, I made three sandwiches.

It's always like this. Last week, there was some cream cheese that Michelle or someone must have thought would go bad since it hadn't been refrigerated overnight, so they threw it away. Perfectly good cream cheese, right into the trashcan. When no one was watching, I pulled it out of the garbage and spread it on some bread I had brought for lunch. It tasted just like cream cheese, only warmer.

This last time, as Abraham was asking me a question about the house's wiring, he went upstairs to flip a switch so that I could see what he was talking about. While he was gone and I was alone, I walked as deliberately and as casually as I knew how to the pile in their garage, and in one lithe motion bent down, picked up the bike light, tested it to see if it worked, and placed it in my pocket.

When Abraham came back out to the garage he said, "See what I'm talking about?"

I said I wasn't sure. "We should really look at it in the daylight with the garage door open."

"Yeah," Abraham said, "you're probably right. Let's get another beer. It's cold out here."

After I rode Marie to her house and got home later, I put new batteries in the light and kept turning it off and on. I had liberated it and brought it back into the realm of working items.

If there is a hell, I'm willing to bet that it is full of refrigerators and mechanical pencils that don't work anymore. Hell is a place where everything looks like it works just fine, but doesn't. This way Lucifer gets the last laugh, because he watches you from behind a stalagmite when you go to use the scissors, but the scissors, as he knows, are too dull to even cut a piece of paper. The paper just sort of folds over limply in the grasp of the blunt blades, leaving a crease where there should have been a cut.

# 8

I REALLY WILL have to buy new pedals soon. These bearings have gotten old and rotten and sometimes even stick in place as I'm rolling, which is never a good situation, since my foot sometimes gets trapped in the toe basket as the crank arms keep rotating.

I ride a bicycle with a fixed gear, which means I can't coast, so it's a problem if my feet become ensnared in crunchy pedals that don't rotate correctly. My bike isn't one of those sporty types, though, with tiny handlebars and flashy rainbow coloring, like so many young people ride these days. It's just a regular bike with a fixed gear. It came that way when I bought it a few years ago, after I maxed everything out and sold my car and moved here and started trying to understand where things went wrong.

I used to have a second set of pedals like the ones that have now gotten old, but since my pedals were working well at the time and I had no complaints about their performance, I sold the second set. The guy I sold them to came by my apartment to pick them up before work. "Thanks!" he said. "I've been looking for some like this for a long time."

"No problem," I said. "Enjoy."

As he walked through the grass toward his car I felt good. *One in, one out*, I thought. But after a second or two of repeating this in my head, I realized it didn't actually work in this situation. What I think I meant was, *Done and done*, because with the twenty dollars I made from him, I'd paid the electricity bill.

After the man drove off in his car with some pedals that worked just fine, I stood there for a little while and looked at the weeds in the space between the sidewalk and the street. *I really should have pulled those*, I thought. But I hadn't, and they'd already gone to seed.

# 9

LAST NIGHT we were eating dinner when out of the blue Marie said she might get a car.

I had brought the previous weekend's newspaper over and we were reading it together while we ate. Marie had made soup with vegetables in it. She's very healthy. Healthier than me, for sure.

There are lots of automobile advertisements in the sports section, but Marie doesn't read that part of the paper, so I wondered what made her bring it up. One of the things I like most about Marie is that she doesn't have a car.

She took a spoonful of soup, held it close to her lips, and blew on it. Before she took a bite, she said, "It could really come in handy to have one, I think."

"That's true," I said. Her mouth is very beautiful. She has small lips and wide white teeth. She's also an excellent kisser. While I answered her, though, I was wondering if I would still love Marie if she owned a car. I wanted to think so, but I wasn't sure. Cars are expensive and take a lot of money to upkeep. It's easy to get parking tickets when you own a car in a city whose revenue streams are under duress. Flat tires are also costly to repair.

When I had a car, I often tried to do many errands in one outing. I would make a little map and a list in my planner of the places I needed to go, and in what order. "Today's plan of action," I called it, after which I put brackets around that phrase as a title, like this:

[Today's Plan of Action]

Since it was the title of the list, I didn't think I needed a colon after it, or underlining or italics. Just the brackets, with the items centered underneath with little boxes I drew to the left so that I could check them off once I had completed them.

☒ Get ready (shower, dishes)
☒ Bank (deposit check)
☒ Store (milk, eggs, lettuce, almonds)

I still make these lists, even though I don't have a car anymore. Having a list as a cyclist may actually be more important than having a list as a driver. If you don't plan your route very well as a bicyclist, you can end up riding miles out of your way while making sure all the errands get done so that you feel good about your day before you fall asleep.

Sometimes nowadays I'll intentionally *not* put the errands in the most energy-saving order possible, though—by running them in different parts of the city out of order, it helps me stay toned, which, as I mentioned earlier, I want to do. Fatness is just little bags of energy that have been saved up and not spent. If I need to get somewhere, then, and I have this energy inside of me that needs to be used, it seems smart to use my bicycle to do so. I have some bags stored on the lower shelves of my torso that I haven't spent yet, but Marie hasn't mentioned them, which is nice of her.

When I had a car I also tried to maximize the amount of time and money I could get out of a parking meter. It was dissatisfying when money was left on a meter even though I'd finished my errands. I liked to exhaust every minute on the meter, down to zero, at which point I could calmly drive off in a moment of perfect stasis.

One of the worst parts about driving was how even short trips were full of things that could go wrong. There were so many obstacles in the way of a stress-free trip. You might, for example, come out and see a thin-papered citation waving in the wind at you from its place under the curbside windshield wiper. It's difficult to have a good day if you don't keep track of the meter minutes correctly, and end up incurring a useless fine. More than anything, parking tickets indicate a personal failure to keep time. That's another thing my dad used to say.

I was thinking about all this as Marie thumbed through the newspaper. "So," she said, looking up at me after reading a little in silence. "What do you think?"

I put Sports down and started looking for Arts. "I'm not sure," I said. On the cover of Arts there was a picture of a band dressed in Amish-looking clothes. They seemed wholesome and sad. One band member wore a wool hat, which I wished I had. It was plain colored and practical. Then I said, "The world profits quite a bit off people's inability to do things correctly."

Marie looked at me for a second. "What does that mean?"

"Parking tickets." I said. "Lapsed registration. Speeding."

"But we could go to the ocean."

I couldn't actually recall the last trip I'd made to the ocean. "I haven't been to the ocean in a long time," I said.

"It would be romantic," Marie said. She touched my arm lightly and ran her fingers through my arm hair, kneading softly.

*Terrible idea*, I thought, *getting a car when we both live in a perfectly walkable and bikeable city*. But I didn't want to ruin the mood. Besides, I do like the ocean.

We ate peacefully and had a fairly nice evening together, sitting by Marie's fireplace. After she touched my arm she didn't say anything more about cars, but something balled up at the top of my stomach below my heart and stayed there most of the evening and into the night.

If Marie gets a car, I don't know what I'll do. I'll still just have my bike.

# 10

Some days it's hard to believe I'm riding on a cushion of air.

It's difficult to conceive of how someone once thought to trap air in a round rubber tube inside of another rubber tube, around a perfect circle of metal. Of course, riding on tires pumped full of air makes sense now, in retrospect, since it's already been invented. But as I'm pedaling along on a straight quiet road, like I was this morning, that idea still seems entirely amazing.

The homeless man with the dinosaurs was awake today when I rode by.

"Morning," I said.

"Sure is," he said. Then he looked at my feet. "Wow. Nice socks."

"Nice dinosaurs."

"They're not real. They're just toys."

"I understand," I said. "Well, I'm off to work."

"Be safe," the homeless man said.

When I got to the office I went straight into the bathroom, because there I can wash my face and hands and towel off. Greg often remarks that riding my bicycle is not a very professional method of transportation, and he's probably right. He likes to point out when I have sweat coming from my eyebrows in the morning, or when the back of my shirt is untucked. It sometimes does that, ratchets itself up my back under my bag as I'm getting to the office. I don't get too close to Greg anymore. I try to stand a few feet away. To save money, I have started making my own deodorant, and it's not working as well as I had hoped. It's just baking soda and cornstarch mixed with a few drops of cologne. I found the cologne in a free pile in front of a house on a walk back from the park. It's called Arete. You have to understand that this cologne was perfectly fine and totally free. But just between you and me, my homemade powdery mixture doesn't really eliminate odor as effectively as it might if I bought it from a store. I'll probably go back to buying deodorant as soon as I can. Good, natural deodorant that doesn't cause Alzheimer's disease and whatever else they say antiperspirant gives you nowadays.

In the bathroom I used cold water to cool my face, letting the drops run fully through my short beard, also getting tiny handfuls up onto my head. The water on my head felt good and cooled me off from the ride, but it's also necessary to make it look like I haven't ridden my bike to work once I've dried off.

Today, though, the paper towel dispenser didn't work. I stood there, waving my hands at the plastic box mounted on the wall. It could not care less that my hands and face and head were wet and that I needed to get into the office for our weekly meeting. I waved more energetically. Then I moved my body from side to side, something like a lindy hop, but still nothing came out in the way of paper towels. I kept waving, though, because that's what the little sign says to do: *Wave hands and towel will dispense.* But the towel wouldn't dispense, and there was no other way to dry off, so I hit the machine with a limp fist.

There was nothing else to do, so I tried to air dry by making jazz hands at myself in the mirror.

Then the door opened and Greg came in.

"Whoa, hey," he said. He was wearing khaki pants and a blue shirt with a green tie. His hair was gelled over and he had a lanyard around his neck. His picture ID rested on his belly.

"Morning, Greg," I said.

"What'd you do, take a shower in here?"

"Just a good splash of water in the morning, you know."

"You're all wet."

"This thing doesn't work," I said. I waved my hand under

the plastic box again. With a slow mechanical sound, one paper towel unrolled.

Greg laughed. "Looks like you fixed it."

"I guess." I yanked the paper towel once it stopped unwinding. As I did so it ripped in half, leaving me with a small square of rough pulp with which to dry myself.

Then Greg headed toward the stall. He closed the door behind him and I could hear his lanyard jangling as he undid his belt. "Didn't you wear that sweater yesterday?" he asked, his voice echoing in the stall.

It was true—I did and do sometimes wear my brown sweater a few times in the same week, but it's not a problem. It's a nice sweater. I have only a few sweaters to choose from and so I'll double up sometimes in the span of just a few days. Like unread books, having too many pieces of clothing hanging in my closet that I don't wear makes me uncomfortable. Plus, when you only work part time and have to pay rent, utilities, insurance, and over $450 in back credit card bills, it doesn't leave a lot for new sweaters. "This one?" I said, looking at my chest.

"Clean up a little, huh?" I could hear his pee streaming loudly into the toilet bowl. I wondered why he hadn't just used the urinal. "Meeting starts in ten."

"Yeah," I said. "See you in a few." I went back to my desk and grabbed my jacket. I took it down to the fourth floor bathroom and rubbed it hard on my head, not even bothering with the paper towels.

# 11

I've become really interested in time. It's fascinating, where all the time goes.

I've also thought a lot about saving time. Well, not really "saving" it, per se, but not losing it, especially on things I don't want to be spending it on, like telephone conversations and traffic.

Tell you the truth, I've been thinking a lot about saving other things too, and what I'm not saving, or why I'm saving what I'm saving. I used to have eleven or twelve shelves full of books, for example—books with impressive logos at the bottoms of their spines. I still have quite a few of those books, but not the ones that I hadn't read but kept around anyway, like a twenty-five cent copy of Alexander Pope's poetry.

The other week Marie pulled it down from the shelf. "Is

this good?" she asked. She thumbed the pages close to her nose with her eyes closed.

"Well," I said. But then I changed the subject to something about how great aged paper and libraries smell, because I've never read that book, but I've owned it for, God, let's see, almost nine years. I've moved it around sometimes, when I was rearranging my books according to genre or height or author, or cleaning, or just browsing my own library looking for a particular monograph, but I've never read it. Not even one page. I bought it right after college, but long after I had forgotten the point of "The Rape of the Lock." It was very cheap and I thought to myself, *A smart man would own this book and read it at night when it is quiet.*

# 12

---

THIS MORNING when I arrived at work there was already a man at the bike rack. There is only one bike rack near the office, and he was parking his bike on the same side, in the same direction as I usually park mine.

"Nice looking bike there," the man said as I approached.

He must work in one of the other buildings, because I've never seen him before. The bike he had locked up looked like it could race at Daytona. It was all sleek curves and precision componentry and probably as light as one gold coin. Very colorful, too. His helmet looked specially made. It even matched his biking jersey, which matched his biking shorts.

My pants don't match anything.

"Oh," I said. "Thanks."

"Yeah, real nice steel frame," he said, stepping back as

if to get a panoramic view. Then he stepped up again and squeezed my brake levers a few times, that universal gesture of trying out a parked bicycle. "You ride every day?"

"From just over the river," I said.

"Even when the weather's shitty? Can't get myself to do it. No, sir," he said. "Hate the rain too much."

"It's not so bad once you're used to it."

"No car, or what?" he asked.

"Not anymore, no."

"That's hardcore," he said. "What'd you pay for it, the bike? If you don't mind me asking."

"Not too much. I just looked around for a while and found it a few years ago."

"Very cool," he said, looking back and forth between my bike's two wheels. As though he wanted to talk about something more, he gestured to my seat, but then pulled his hand back and picked up his waterproof bag. "Well," he said, "take care."

"You, too," I replied.

I pretended to start to lock up, fidgeting with my cable and whatnot as he walked away, but when he was around the corner and out of sight, I went across the street and down a few blocks and locked up to a light pole.

# 13

On nights that I can't sleep I go outside and ride around the city.

My bills are due soon. I'm a light sleeper, so if something wakes me up I usually can't fall back asleep, because I'm thinking about the bills.

If it's cold, I button several shirts over each other until a neat origami flower of triangular shirt collars blossoms at my chest. I also wear wool mittens. The left one has a growing hole around the fingers because it got snagged on my brake lever and I don't know how to mend it.

For night riding, I keep all my lights as bright and alert as possible. The new one I got from Abraham's garage is the brightest light I have. I keep the lights refreshed with a rotation of new batteries. In my arsenal of illumination I have three white blinking lights in front, and now two rear lights that flash in their own distinct pattern. Regular style (blink-blink, blink-blink, blink-blink) and Abraham style (blink-blink-BLINK, blink-blink-BLINK, blink-blink-BLINK).

My apartment is up a steep flight of stairs, but I've found a way to successfully ascend and descend the narrow stairwell with my bike on my shoulder. The front wheel points down toward my knees so that I can easily get into and out of doorways just by turning the handlebars as if I were riding. The rear wheel is positioned above and behind my head. The saddle rests near my right ear.

It feels nice when the bike itself is part of my body. With appendages of aluminum and rubber and leather and steel like this, you would expect me to run into things that branch out into my path. But I move dexterously, without running into anything, because I practice going up and down the stairs so often. This is important to me because I'm able to leave when there are bills to pay without waking Kim and Doug, who live downstairs. They don't wake me up, so I don't want to wake them up, either. It's a little test I give myself. *Can you do it again? You know they're asleep and they'll hear you if you're too loud. Can you navigate this gauntlet without banging the wall or snagging your spokes on the door handle?* Silence and fluidity are demanded of me, but I usually pass the test.

On the ride tonight, my bicycle body felt better than it has in a while. My wheels made a spry sound on the moist pavement, and the whole atmosphere was clean and soft. I slipped between its particles with very little effort. On certain nights like tonight, the molecules hang out more casually, loosening their bonds with one another, not taking their job of being the air too seriously.

I do this thing sometimes on my bike that must make me appear drunk, even though I'm not, and I did it tonight. It's a gliding, swooping pattern I set myself to, like skiing downhill, or like a giant brass pendulum swinging in its wooden case: I let the weight of my body on the rotating wheels create a slight momentum that I control and perpetuate by dipping back and forth. My pedals keep moving, even if I'm not pedaling, and so the experience is one in which I waltz down the road as I dip to the left and then right in a rhythmic lunging act. I feel like a matador: the bull comes straight at you and if you are going to get the audience to love you, you have to get as close as possible to the angry animal while artfully stepping to the side as it charges past your deep red cape.

So I did this.

I rode straight toward every manhole cover in the road. I saw the slippery discs up ahead as I cruised, so I dipped myself to and fro as I approached, and at the last physical second I pushed the lower part of my body out from under me to the right before the manhole. Then, I simultaneously leaned left with my torso to cause the bike to make a gorgeous unbroken arc around the wet object and then back underneath me again as I straightened up on the other side, unscathed.

I rode for about two hours this way. I didn't really go anywhere. I just rode in circles around the neighborhood.

Eventually, I was sleepy again. Just as when I came down, I passed the test going up the stairs, and fell asleep just fine.

# 14

I was released from work early today because there was a fire in our building and everyone had to evacuate. I'm not sure what caused the fire, or if there were even flames associated with the situation, because I didn't see it.

According to Michelle, something happened on the eleventh floor, but we work on the fifth, so we all just went outside and stood around for a while and then Greg told us we were free to go. "Lost cause, folks," he said. There was no smoke that I could see, and there was only one fire truck and five firemen. They didn't seem to be in a hurry. "This could take all afternoon, so I'll just see you guys tomorrow," Greg said. He's never let us leave early before.

Since I had brought my bag with me—exactly like they say you shouldn't do when a fire alarm goes off—I just walked down the block to the light pole and rode home.

It was a pleasant enough ride until I got over the river. After the bridge, a gentleman on a noisy, portly bike continued to pull in front of me at stop signs and stoplights, even though I was the faster rider. Why he thought that was a particularly good idea, I'm not sure. It certainly didn't make any sense to me. Sometimes he didn't stop at all. I watched several motorists brake for him even though they had the right-of-way. So he kept ending up ahead of me, which I wouldn't mind if he were quicker. But as it was, I had to go around him.

I felt bad.

I wasn't racing. That's not what I was looking to do. The physics and momentum inherent to our riding styles and dissimilar setups, though, made it so that I would inevitably go faster sooner and longer than him, but he didn't understand. I passed him seven times in twenty blocks before he veered off into the park. During our ride together he never once acknowledged that, hey, that's the guy I keep pulling in front of every time we stop. Not a "Oh, sorry about that," or "Nice day, huh?" or "Hop, hop, ho, hup!" Nothing. He just kept riding each time as if I wasn't there. I thought I was showing him the courtesies of the road, but he didn't even notice me.

I'm not invisible, though, right? Please tell me that you can see me.

Further along, I was passed by a car with doors that open like a space shuttle. It may have been a Lamborghini, but it seems unlikely that anyone in this city would be nonchalantly driving a Lamborghini around on a normal afternoon in which my workplace apparently caught fire. Perhaps it was just a very fast Honda.

When I got home, I should have gotten a jump on my exercises, but since on Tuesdays and Thursdays I'm usually at work all the way until five, I thought maybe I'd instead use the time to jot down some thoughts I've been having. I tried to make it as brief and professional as possible.

*Hello. My name is Nicholas Allander and should you be able to spare them, I would like a few moments of your time to tell you about safer cycling. One item of note is that expensive cars are attractive, but my advice is to be wary of them. They come in sleek and appealing colors and usually have powerful engines. Sporty automobiles share this characteristic and are often designed and manufactured to go upwards of 200 miles per hour—not unlike actual racecars that run on high-grade fuel—which they really are capable of going, even in residential neighborhoods in which the speed limit is almost exclusively 25. Owners of expensive and sporty cars have been known to enjoy showing other people that their cars are expensive and sporty by:*

+ *taking tight turns*
+ *making unpredictable bursts of speed in confined areas*
+ *squealing their tires*

+ *honking and shouting exclamations out the window*
+ *passing cyclists or other cars very closely*

That's what I've been thinking. And given that I was put into a sort of racing situation on my way home, I was also thinking about how a few years ago my friend Brett encouraged me to try bike racing. For my first race he loaned me an expensive mountain bike because he had more than one. It was a short race that went in dirt circles for about twenty minutes, which I enjoyed, sort of, until I rounded the final lap and went off the course into the weeds. The green vines got grossly tangled in my rear gear cluster, so I picked up the bike and threw it as far off the course as I could and then walked across the finish line.

The sun is going down now and I still haven't exercised. That's disappointing. I didn't take full advantage of the afternoon. I know I only work part time and can exercise later, but there is something exhilarating about using unexpected time off to be productive. Instead, I've just been sitting here at my desk, thinking.

My bike's propped up against the wall where I left it when I got in. It's leaning there quietly, its handlebars tilted drowsily to one side. Like a sleeping horse.

It's dark now and I'm tired.

# 15

It was raining this morning, so I went out and smoked a cigarette on the front porch. I took my coffee out there, too, and watched the cold drops slide easily over everything.

The first time I smoked a cigarette was with some coworkers one night after we had had drinks at a martini bar. I don't even know why I said I would join them for a smoke, but when someone passed me the cigarette, I just put it between my fingers and to my mouth and sucked in and then blew out. I didn't cough, but then someone said, "Hey, Nick. Have you ever smoked before?"

"Sure I have," I said.

"Oh, okay," they said.

I noticed, sitting on the porch, that the hanging airplane plant above the outdoor table could probably use some water, so I took it down and put it out in the grass. It was pretty clear to me that the plant was already dead, but perhaps the water getting down in there, into the soil and roots, could revive it. Then I sat back down.

I inhaled slowly. The cigarette rested easily on my lips. Then I exhaled. The smoke came up out of my mouth and lingered around my head before it dissipated into the rainy air. It was hard to tell if the morning was foggy or if what I saw was just my smoke. Everything was gray, though, one way or another.

My mom used to get up and smoke cigarettes and drink coffee when I was a kid. Then she would come up into my room to wake me up. Her breath was that thick breath of smoky caffeination, or caffeinated smokiness. "Time to get up, Nick," she'd say, bending over my bed to kiss me on the forehead. Every morning, when I heard her knee popping as she came up the stairs, I would crawl as far under the covers as I could. It's not that I didn't want to get up. It's that I hated the smell of coffee and cigarettes first thing every morning.

Once she asked, "Why don't you let me kiss you anymore?" Instead of doing what I should have done, which was lie and say I was just sleepy, I told her the truth. "Your breath's terrible," I said. "Like an ashtray."

Then she cried.

I was probably nine or ten.

Every day after that she woke me up from the doorframe of my room. "Time to get up, Nick," she would say, instead of coming in and bending over me like she used to. I told myself that when I grew up I would never drink coffee or smoke, both of which I guess I do now anyway.

I just kept sitting outside in the raininess with my coffee and cigarette. In addition to a train yard, a glass factory, and a small cement plant, I live near the large corporate headquarters of a grocery store. My rent is affordable because this part of the city is muddy and industrial.

People were driving by on their way to work. Instead of using the wider and faster road one block to the north of my apartment that other drivers use during their commute—and which is therefore trafficky—many of the corporate grocery store employees use my small street as a shortcut. A shortcut fails to be a shortcut, though, when the road is narrow and rife with stop signs. A short cut is also not a short cut when a majority of everyone uses it.

I wished I had a radar gun. As my cigarette burned down I thought about how fast these people were going. From my vantage point on the porch they seemed to be in actual competition. Speed is violent, like heat can be, or intelligence, and so I wished I could go out on the street and hold a sign that said something like, "Slow down, please!" with a picture of a thumbs-down.

I didn't make or hold up a sign, though, because these people were in a hurry to get to work. Instead, I closed my eyes. I tried to forget the drivers and not care about how they were driving, just like Marie has told me I should do. I also tried not to think about what they eat for lunch or how they afford it.

Drinking coffee and smoking a cigarette with your eyes closed is a lot like communing with people you've never met, or who are dead. This morning, trying not to think about cars, I thought of smoking with Miles Davis.

I took one more deep drag of my cigarette and then crushed it in the ashtray.

# 16

Good morning.

It's very early and I just had the most beautiful ride across the city in the dark. I'm sitting on the bed now drinking coffee from my Sleeping Beauty mug. It's a deep bowl decorated with the Princess talking to the forest animals, and has a slim but comfortable handle. Like the cologne with which I made my deodorant, I found the mug in a free box on the street.

One of the cats just brought me a moth in his mouth that he must have hunted down outside. He thinks that it's a gift for me to receive, a moth. There is pride in his large eyes. I can see it. I don't have the heart to explain to him that moths are probably more something he likes than me. He's looking around the blanket for a place to ball up and sleep away the rest of the morning now that he's accomplished his cat-task of bringing me a moth.

Last night Marie invited me over. Her living room is full of plush chairs and couches that together face a fireplace. I like it there. I feel relaxed, and not worried about the usual things: when I'll get paid; whether my clothes are appropriate; where I should lock up; whether my pants will get caught in the gears.

The atmosphere around Marie is easy and calm, like a different dimension than the one I live in. She has made wiser decisions with her life than I have. For one, she has been employed full time for several years as a kindergarten teacher. She's younger than me, but seems so much farther ahead. No one lives below or above her, and she maintains a small garden in her backyard. Marie doesn't spend a lot of money, but never seems in need of anything, either.

On a few of our recent dates, I've told Marie about the taxes I owe this year. Marie is the kind of person who is supportive and patient no matter what your goal is. I've also told her about the debt I've been repaying and that I'm getting close to eliminating it completely. I explained that it's taken me a long time and that I see the world differently now.

Yesterday, I gave her a call. On the telephone I told her that I had sold a few more books, got paid from my job at Stevens', and was done paying off my taxes. In her teacher voice, she said, "I believe, Mr. Allander, this is a cause to celebrate."

"I concur," I said.

Then she invited me over.

When I arrived at her house, she opened the front door.

"Well, what a surprise," she said, pretending she didn't know I was coming. Then she laughed lightly and I could see her beautiful teeth. "Want to bring your bike inside?"

"Sure," I said. Out of habit, I threw it up on my shoulder and ducked in the doorway. I could smell some sort of baking bread, and what I thought was stew.

"Want a beer?" she asked, and I said that I did.

When Marie came back from the kitchen and I had set my bike out of the way down the hall, we sat in the living room together. Before she took her seat, she leaned over and kissed me on the cheek.

"So," she said, pulling her legs up underneath her in the chair, "you've paid them off in full?"

I took a slow pull from my beer. "Finally. But it still feels stupid."

"What does?"

"Not having been able to pay them in the first place."

"Lots of people can't pay their taxes right away. That's why they have payment plans."

"Yeah," I said. "But I don't want to be one of those people."

Marie slowly lifted her glass of wine in my direction.

"Here's to being who you want to be, then."

It really was a nice evening. Blurry and peaceful. After I finished my beer and we sat down to dinner, we drank the whole bottle of wine that Marie said she was saving for a special occasion.

At 4 a.m. I woke up suddenly next to Marie. *Shit*, I thought. *My alarm.*

"Marie," I said, lightly shaking her leg. "I didn't turn off my alarm before I came over."

"Okay," she said sleepily.

I laid my hand on her shoulder. "I have to go turn it off."

She didn't answer. She wrapped her arms tightly around me.

"It won't turn off on its own," I said. "It just keeps going."

She rolled over.

"Marie." I touched her hair. "I have to go turn off my alarm."

"What alarm?" she said.

"The one at my house. It'll wake up Kim and Doug downstairs."

"You have an alarm clock?"

"You know that. You've seen it."

"I don't know," she said.

"It's really loud," I whispered. "And it's Saturday."

She was breathing heavily. I looked around the bedroom in the dark. I could barely make out anything. I imagined my pants and shirt were still folded on the chair in the corner where I left them.

"Hey, Marie," I said softly. I shook her leg again. "I have to go."

"What? What time is it?"

"Thanks for having me. It was wonderful."

"Where're you going?"

"My alarm's going to go off. It's not fair to wake them up."

"Who?"

"Doug and Kim."

"Just stay," she said. My eyes had adjusted to the dark a little, so I could see that her eyes were still closed.

"No, listen. I'd hate it if someone left their alarm blaring when they weren't there."

"Don't go," Marie said, sighing.

"I have to," I said quietly.

I kissed her on the forehead and then on the mouth. She didn't say anything else and didn't rustle, so I slipped out of bed and then out the door.

It's not easy to leave a naked woman alone in a comfortable bed, but once I was riding, I didn't want to stop. There were no cars anywhere on the road. My bike was almost silent. In just the small stretch of night city I saw:

+ the lights of the bridge reflect on the water
+ a fully grown man asleep in a bush
+ a family of raccoons wobbling around a trashcan
+ the moon shining through thin clouds

Everything was quiet. *I'm doing the right thing*, I thought.

When you ride at night under large street lamps, something happens with your shadow. Because you're moving and passing directly beneath the streetlights in series, your shadow sneaks up behind you and then emerges out from under your tires. It does this in a totally natural and elegant motion, pulls right out in front of you as though you are constantly getting passed by different versions of yourself. This happens under every light, over and over again in a secret visual rhythm.

Since there was no traffic, I didn't stop at any lights. I was able to ride for entire blocks without looking up, just watching my silhouette sashay along the empty streets. I was seeing myself ride, the shape of my body and my head in my helmet. My legs moved up and down. Up and down. Up and down.

But if you look carefully, it's not just one shadow that makes up your entourage, but three or four or five, because other lights are also competing to cast a likeness of your being on the ground. At any one point, you can have your long competitive shadow moving out in front of you—the one that you'll never really catch—but also a slower one to your left, and then another misshapen one to your right, and a few more behind you that you probably won't ever see in your lifetime unless you learn to ride your bike facing backward.

When I got home I turned off my alarm and thought about going back to sleep. But instead I just decided to brew coffee and wake up. It was just me and the curled cat and the dead moth and the Sleeping Beauty forest animals, together in the early morning, thinking about Marie.

# 17

At a very busy intersection on the way to work this morning there was a grown man dressed as a mattress. His arms protruded out of the thin sides of the costume, but his elbows were still inside. His hands waved furiously at me as I rode up in the bike lane.

In an automobile you are shielded from your fellow commuters, as well as any other entity that might be in the street or on the sidewalk or beside you in some capacity. But on a bike you are within talking distance without any glass or metal between you. That forces you to contend with the reality, for example, that someone is dressed like a bedroom accessory while holding a large sign that reads, "50% off all month at McGuire's!"

Anyway, the light was red and we were right next to each other. People in their cars looked straight ahead. The morning clouds were breaking up and the rain seemed like it was going to stay on the other side of the hill. The man's hands were still excited and moving, but his face was unsmiling.

I didn't know what else to do, so I said, "How is it today?"

"Been better," he answered. "Need a mattress?"

"I'm okay," I said, "but maybe later."

The light turned green, so I started to pedal.

"Sales all week," the mattress called after me.

# 18

---

THIS MORNING was a good morning. The rain I heard coursing through the gutter all night like little marbles thumping down a cardboard tube seemed to stop right before I pulled myself to the side of the bed and put my feet on the floor, pointed toward the kitchen.

To make further strides in the efficiency of my routine, I decided to ready the coffee pot last night so as to not have to try to piece together all the odds and ends of brewing while wrapped in a gauze of morning sleepiness. I did this slowly before bed, reveling in the precision and the prescience of my actions. I first scrubbed the inside of the glass pot for many minutes. Holding the pot on my hand like a huge glass mitten, I spun it around on the sponge, trying to get any old burned coffee out of the curves of the bottom. After it was rinsed, I measured out the exact amount of water and poured it carefully into the chamber in the back of the brewer. I pulled a single filter from the infinite nest of other filters. Then I delicately shoveled two and a half scoops of coffee grounds into the thin paper crucible. In one sinuous motion I placed the full filter into its sieve, closed the lid of the brewer, and wiped the whole thing clean. I was ahead of time and it felt nice.

So when I stepped out of bed and shuffled toward the coffeepot this morning, all I had to do was push the button. The brewer gurgled and chugged in spits and spats. Little puffs of steam came out from around the sides of the lid.

I leaned against the sink with my arms crossed. In a sweeping look, I surveyed my cupboards as slowly as I had put the coffee together. Everything was in place. The reused mayonnaise and jelly jars, from which I had peeled their original labels under the hot running faucet, were in a neat line, more or less half full of pasta and nuts. The few old cookbooks I got when my mother passed away were stacked from biggest on bottom to smallest on top. Most of their recipes call for ingredients I can't afford.

Then I had a really good idea.

I've never understood how I'm supposed to get all the honey, which I prefer over sugar in my coffee, all the way out of the bear. There's always honey residue left all over the inside of it that, no matter how long I store it upside-down, never comes out. But when the coffee was done and

I had my mug set up to the side with a dollop of milk, instead of pouring the coffee directly into the porcelain, I poured it first into the honey bear. Then I swished it all around. The swishing caused a hot mini coffee typhoon inside the bear, and with every rotation it took more and more of the hiding honey off the plastic sides. After the hot coffee swirled around and forced the hardened honey into liquid, there was only a half-cup of sweetened coffee inside the honey bear, which I poured over the milk in my mug. Then the honey bear was truly empty and I put it in the recycle bin.

# 19

Today, for no good reason I stood up on my pedals and pretended to whip my bicycle like a jockey would a horse.

It was not as cool as I thought it was going to be this morning, which meant that I sweated again, heavily—so much so that my collar was wet almost out to its tips by the time I got to work. I bundled too thoroughly in proportion to the exertion I expended. It's a delicate algorithm, one I may never completely master. It's embarrassing, but I compensate by getting in a little early, so that after I've rinsed and toweled off, my collar and hair have a reasonable head start on drying before Michelle and the others arrive. This also lessens the chance that folks will comment on my appearance. I don't need extra attention. I just want to count and record the checks, slim down, and maybe sip some beer in the evenings out on the porch without thinking too much about money.

My sweatiness today was also compounded by the fact that my crank fell off my bike on the hill before the bridge. Why it did that exactly I don't know. It could have had something to do with the jockeying, but I doubt it. I don't think I'm strong enough to tear the pedal and entire crank mechanism right out of the bottom bracket, do you? My thighs are getting stronger, I think, even if my midsection lags in visually boasting the results of my commute, but I'm hardly capable of shearing metal components in half. Firm, like small firewood logs, are these two legs. But my belly, bless it, is still just a bag of ashes.

According to my calculations, last month I rode 182 miles, burning 8,575 calories, though when I stand naked in the mirror and look at my torso from different angles, I can't really tell. Maybe one gets fit from the inside out, and for now the fitness is happening beneath my skin and in my legs, and soon it will start to show around the equator. My stomach is what Marie rests her hand on when she sleeps wrapped around me from behind, which is why I want so badly to do right by that part of my body.

Maybe my mirror is a trick mirror. I should pedal harder.

The thing about trying to exercise to feel better about yourself and impress someone you love is that you don't really know you're fit until you are. There's no in between, unless you use all sorts of fancy scales and tracking mechanisms and charts and trainers, which of course I don't have. Unless you count the mirror.

Anyway, at the intersection before the bridge, right as some of the few other people who also ride their bicycles to work like me—we're usually gathered together in a quiet bunch—had lined up at the light and were awaiting our turn to climb the tiny hill that would take us over the river and into downtown, where we each conceivably sort checks or answer phones or call people or tell other people to call people about important things, the debacle with my bike went down.

I like that word. *Debacle*. I even looked it up. "The tumultuous break up of ice in a river." I can understand that. A mass of heavy frozen water cracking and crashing as it breaks free and floats away on its own, untethered from the constraints of the rest of the fettered flow.

As I jumped off the line, though—without making it *seem* like I was jumping off of the line—I got in a good three or four pedal strokes before

— *WHISH!* —

my whole crank fell off the right side of my bike. It broke free of its own volition and parted ways with me and the bike to which it had been attached for many years. It took me a second to discover what had happened, but I coasted to a stop as everyone passed by without saying anything, and then I pulled myself up onto the sidewalk. *Huh*, I thought.

Without the necessary replacement bolt on hand or in my bag—I hadn't thought of carrying extra bolts—I could do nothing but walk my bike the rest of the way to the office, holding the greasy chain in my hand so that it wouldn't drag behind me like an oily dead snake. I made it to the office in good time, which surprised me. I've always figured having strong bicycle legs doesn't quite equal having strong walking legs, but as I've explained, I'm not a scientist, so maybe it does.

The rest of the day didn't go very well, either. Greg called me into his office this afternoon and talked to me a while with the door closed.

The first time a boss ever called me into his office was when I was working at a pizza place, and I walked in thinking I might get a raise or maybe get asked to do a special project. But instead I got fired for repeatedly putting too much cheese on the pizzas, which was costing the restaurant "more than my monthly salary." I wasn't on salary, though—I was hourly, a fact I decided not to point out as I left.

Much like the boss who fired me, Greg is not a bad man. He just appreciates certain qualities I do not possess.

"Heya, Nick," he said about an hour after I ate my lettuce and nuts outside. "Can you come in here a minute?"

"Sure," I said.

"How's it going out there?" he said, closing the door behind us.

On the wall behind his desk Greg had a large framed poster of some old masons building a house or a small factory in a place that looked a lot like London. "Well," I said, getting lost for a moment among the workers of Greg's poster. I very much liked their wood-handled tools with triangular metal blades for smoothing and removing excess mortar. Four men, each in various suspenders and different versions of the same wool cap, went about their individual tasks. The gentleman worker in the foreground was my favorite. More so than the others, he was truly concentrating on doing a fine job, even if from the outside the work looked simplistic and mundane: *swipe, plop*. But what brilliant strokes. *Swish, swoosh. Swish, shoosh.* With the soft *J* of a hand movement, he was bringing this wall into beautiful architectural completion, one small brick at a time. "Well," I said again, "lots of invoices recently, as you know, but good. As long as I keep all the records straight it goes pretty smoothly."

"Do you remember speaking to Nicola Robins on the telephone last week?" Greg asked.

"I don't think so, no."

"She called about the tiled tub and sink combo, and mentioned talking to you."

"I may have talked to her, then. I don't remember, exactly."

"Well, she called me directly. To complain. She said you were very rude."

"That's interesting," I said.

"The thing is, that's actually not the first time someone has complained about your phone etiquette. Which is why we've been having our little professionalism talks. She said she's taking her business elsewhere."

"But I've even been practicing," I said. "Just the other night I thought through how I would explain to someone who doesn't ride a bicycle what to watch out for on the road. It would sound like this: *Taxicabs are fast moving vehicles.*"

Greg raised his palm to stop me, and then brought the curve of his hand to his mouth and rubbed his cheeks with his thumb and fingers. I wasn't communicating very well. The way I see it, cab drivers enjoy gratuities, and many customers say things like that guy in *Infinite Jest* does: "To the library, and step on it!" So cabbies are inclined, for their own monetary gain, to employ such tactics as speeding, weaving, and other aggressive motoring maneuvers. *Infinite Jest* is one of those books that I'm still vacillating on what to do with, because I haven't finished it. In fact, I haven't even really started, but I haven't sold it either, though it's probably worth half my rent. It's a hardcover first edition. The taxicab and library scene occurs on page ten, which is as far as I've ever gotten on three different tries. But now Wallace is dead. He cashed out when he was on top, just like they tell you to do when you're gambling. People who lose at gambling are those who don't know when to cash out. Despite the fact that they're not doing very well anymore and know it, people just keep going, like Joe Montana or Madonna, intoxicated by their own past success. I lost $40 in Vegas on my first blackjack bet, but Wallace knew what he was doing. Critics only get serious about you after you're gone.

I know a man my age should have some things in place as a foundation, like a career and some investments, or at least a personal trajectory. But I've gained none of these, though I'm certainly working on losing weight. I am, however, gambling that *Infinite Jest* will end up, once I get around to finishing it, being worth its bulk and its imposition on my life as a book I have owned and looked at and moved around for years, but have never actually read.

"You don't have a car, do you?" Greg said.

"I don't, no."

"Does that explain your hands?"

I looked down. "My chain fell off."

Greg looked closely at my fingers, seemingly focused on my fingernails, and then went back to rubbing his cheeks and jaw. "What are you looking for do you think?" he asked.

I looked back up at one of the other workers in the poster. Unlike my favorite, he was sitting behind everyone else, eating lunch and reading a newspaper. "I'm not sure," I said.

"Nothing comes to mind?"

"Not really."

"Your hair. Your shirt," Greg said, waving in my direction.

"The ride was going really well," I started to explain.

"Can you get some new clothes?"

"I think so, yeah."

"What about taking the bus? Is there a route that comes by your place?"

"I don't know. I usually just ride, unless my crank falls off, then I have to walk. But it's not a problem, the biking, is it?"

"Look into the bus schedule," Greg said. "We may even be able to get you a discounted pass."

"The economy—"

"But is Stevens' even where you want to be? I can't honestly say that you look like you enjoy yourself around here. I mean, you're on the margins of the office pretty regularly."

"I can work on that. The margins."

Greg was really going now. "I just wonder what you want out of all this. I have a steady thing here. I go home at night and Rebecca has a nice dinner ready and Holly and Travis are there at the dinner table and tell us about their days at school. I don't make a ton of money, obviously. You know that. Shit, you see the checks. We're a fucking sink company, but we get by, you know? I sleep next to a nice woman and wake up and have breakfast and then come back into this goddamn place all over again, but it's bearable. I just wonder what you've got that you don't want to give up. Part time here is all right, I guess, but there must be something that you look forward to. You're a bright guy."

My favorite worker was still dutifully building his wall. Being able to ride home once I fix my crank arm, that's what I looked forward to. Cutting vegetables. Losing more weight. Kissing Marie. That's all, really.

"Never mind," Greg said. "Forget I said any of that. Truth is, you've got to make it look like you care what's going on around here. Go to lunch with Michelle and Dave once in a while. Blend in. But also think about what makes you happy, and find a way to go get it. If that's not at Stevens', I understand that. We all have to do what we have to do. But if it is, I need you to be a bit more professional, okay?"

"Absolutely."

"That's all I'm asking."

"I know."

"And don't be too hard on yourself. You're good at what you do. I just want you to be okay." He paused. "Happy."

"Thanks, Greg," I said, standing.

"No sweat," he said.

When I sat back down at my desk and looked out the window, I saw six kids riding BMX bikes around our parking lot. The bikes' seats were really low, but the kids never sat on them, so I guess it didn't matter. They took turns riding in circles, speeding up along the blacktop and gaining enough speed to jump up with both wheels onto a thin concrete curb that bordered the far end of the lot.

Being able to jump your bicycle and get both wheels off the ground at the same time is a great skill. I learned how to do it as a child, but it still impresses me every time I see it. The contest, I could tell, was who could ride on that thin curb the farthest, and it seemed they had each decided on a personal strategy for winning. With enough speed, your momentum could take you pretty far. But on the other hand, going slowly and paying careful attention to your balance and pedal strokes could pay off, too. Five of the six went with speed, while with every one of his tries, the last one would hop up onto the curb and ride steadily as far as he could, staring down at the cement tightrope.

I watched them trading high fives and laughs for a while, until Michelle came by and gave me the mail and the day's invoices, so I got back to work. After processing a check or two and entering it into the database, I looked up to see which of the kids might be in the lead, but by that time they had ridden off. I hoped the slow riding boy had won, but it seemed unlikely.

Afterward, contrary to my custom, I said goodbye to everyone in the office. "See you guys tomorrow," I said, sort of too softly for everyone to hear. But I think Greg caught it. Then I walked to the bike shop and bought a new bolt so I could ride home, like I wanted.

# 20

---

Today I saw many items of note on my way to and from the office.

Those things were:

+ five whole slices of pizza on the ground, uneaten, pepperonis still intact

+ a puddle the size of my living room

+ a small dog in a sack

+ a doorman dressed as a medieval court jester

+ one shoe

+ three little birds chasing a much larger bird

+ a man in his car honking at a squirrel

You will not believe me, but over the course of the last several months I've also seen these people commuting by bicycle:

+ a person wearing a full-body snowsuit

+ someone who constantly rides a wheelie

+ a young guy whose commuter bike is a tall unicycle with one knobby tire

After work this afternoon, I bought a bottle of scotch whisky with some money I made off a few first edition books I sold. I did so to help myself out.

A few days after I'd had to turn off my alarm, Marie and I rode our bikes to see an old movie at the cheap theater. It was overcast and the sun was almost down, like a light bulb tucked into a sleeping bag. When we were locking up, I noticed Marie was not using the locking cable I bought her for Christmas last year. It's the same type of cable I use, which costs the equivalent of selling five books at the bookstore, or two on the Internet. As I've said, I like to use both a U-lock and a cable, for extra protection.

"Did you bring your cable?" I asked.

"Yeah, it's in my bag."

"Are you going to take it into the theater with you?"

"I think you make things harder on yourself," Marie said. "It's not your bike. It'll be fine. I promise."

"But your bike's going to fall over if someone locks up next to us. Just use the cable."

"You have to let things go sometimes."

I looked at Marie. Her hair was wavy from the ride over. Even under her helmet, it has a way of getting poofy from the wind while she rides. Like usual, she was dressed nicely, though not impractically, and looked extremely attractive. But here's what I was thinking: there was a cable, and a need for a cable, and time to put the cable into action, and yet Marie was not going to use the cable.

"Seriously, though," I said.

"You know what you can worry about? You can worry about the fact that you left my house the other day in the middle of the night. You want to tell me about that? If you want to worry about something, worry about that."

"What? I told you. I had to turn off my alarm."

"Who does that?"

Marie looked at me hard, as though she really wanted me to answer that question, even though we both already knew the answer. Then she said, "Ready to go in?" I looked at her bike, then at my feet, then up at her, and finally said I was.

Which brings me to the whisky. I've started wondering whether drinking might help me care less about the things I take so seriously, so I bought a bottle of Johnnie Walker Red.

I know that in history many smart and important people have been alcoholics. Right now, then, I'm pairing the whisky with a can of Hamm's. It's what I had in the fridge. Hamm's is not in any way, shape, or form a good beer, nor is Johnnie Walker good scotch, but I make do with what I have.

I'm sitting on the front porch, watching the clouds bunch together and move slowly along the horizon. Here's what I have deduced about clouds from riding my bike each day as well as watching them from the front yard. Foggy clouds are wet, but warm. Rain from dark purple clouds isn't always as uncomfortable as you might think. High faraway clouds that look like the end of a Q-tip pulled off its cardboard shaft mean it's going to be windy. Cloudless days can be cold even though the sun is shining.

Oh, clouds. Johnnie Walker tastes a little bit like that rusty brown water that comes out of your faucet after the water main has been turned off and then on again. I can feel the alcohol in my legs right now. They're all noodly. Now the veins in my neck are warm.

I feel relaxed, but I'm not sure I'm comfortable with how much this whisky costs. Buying things is really just an equation, an equation that many people either forget or decide to ignore for the better part of their adult lives. The first part of that equation goes like this:

Life = Years/Weeks/Days/Hours

My fingers are tingling in a good way.

What I'm trying to say is that our life is usually X number of years long, and those years are composed of weeks, days, hours, and minutes, all just various measurements, of course, of time. This isn't unfamiliar to you. As adult people in a civilized modern society, we usually have to decide what to do with all these hours and days and weeks we have on our hands, since we're alive and the world is spinning and we no longer have to go out and hunt boar with sharp sticks in order to eat. Most of us, then, after graduating high school or college, find ourselves out in the world, confronting the next integer in the equation, which might, for example, involve filing checks for a sink manufacturer:

Years/Weeks/Days/Hours = Work

Here's where things start to get a little sticky and where, unfortunately, some members of society, including me, have fallen off the caboose of responsible progress. This is the part of the equation where we give our life, otherwise known as time, or many of our waking hours, to a workplace. This we do for the most important component in the equation:

Work = Money

Nice, right? With money we can do whatever we want. Who doesn't like money? I can't not like it myself. Would you like a new record to listen to when you are relaxing out on the front porch? Well, then, by all means, with the money that you make from your job, you can go out and buy that record. Perhaps you're lucky enough to already own a record player, too, in which case you're all set to relax. See a new restaurant at which you would like to eat? Your money is also good there.

This monetary arrangement, by most estimations, is a pretty good system of symbolic participation, a system I'm not so much complaining about as I'm in awe of at this precise and loopy moment. Anyway, by this point I've ruined the build-up and already all but spelled out the next part of the equation because I've had too much Johnnie Walker:

Money = Things and Stuff

This is just what it sounds like—food, furniture, hamster cages, Halloween costumes, etc. What people in business refer to as "goods."

Okay, then. Let's recap.

There are two equations I've brought up:

1) Hamm's + Johnnie Walker Red = noodly legs

and

2) Life = Time = Work = Money = Things and Stuff

Whoo wheeee. I'm pretty sure I'm drunk. I'm caring less already. I had not intended to think about money or economic philosophy under the influence, but I suppose some things just happen, so I'm going to go ahead and ride this one out and see where it will take us.

So. Let's for a moment forget the first equation and focus more intently on the second. For things that we want, we spend money, and we make that money by giving up much of the time in our lives at a job. By this reasoning, in the equation I have been explaining in the waning parts of this beautiful evening in which the clouds slowly tumble along, life boils down to and equals Things and Stuff. If this doesn't depress the pants right off you, then you are living in a very deep hole underground or far up in the mountains and I wish you all the best there.

Now here's the thing: you don't need to be depressed just because I have suggested that you should be and because of the fact that I don't have money and that you might, due to whatever smart financial decisions you made in your twenties or thirties in line with the equation above. That would not be fair at all. Nor would it be consistent with the intentions of what I'm trying to do, which, to be completely honest, I'm not really sure of right now, myself.

Three fingers of Johnnie Walker Red, and I've already ridden this Devil-may-care windjammer into the sunset and am miles from shore and think it's time to turn around.

*Feel more. Care less.* A friend of mine told me that once, and I think it's a pretty good idea.

That's all I want to do.

# 21

---

Hardly ever in my life have I attended parties. But one night in college I rode my bike over to a get-together. In between a few chats about bands I'd never heard of, but pretended to, on the back patio I drank about nine Rolling Rocks. I looked for a long time at the way the porch light was hitting the leaves on the trees. Then I decided to head home. In my mind, taking the bike path through the natural area was the safest route. If I rode on established streets I might get a ticket for biking under the influence—a BUI—which is possible. Problem was, I hadn't noticed there weren't any streetlights on this path, mainly because I had only ever taken it during the day. So about 200 yards into the dim park I couldn't see the trail at all.

But I just kept riding anyway. *You can make it*, I thought. *Just keep pedaling. Just keep pedaling.*

It only got darker, though, and when the path turned to the left, I kept riding straight, and wrecked off the trail into a grassy ditch and laid there for who knows how long. The world just spun and spun above and below me.

This morning my head hurt as though I had tried to ramp my bike up a curb and fell face-first onto the sidewalk. It's Saturday, so I was just going to lay there for a while, but then Marie called and asked if I wanted to go for a walk. I said I did. My stomach was rolling. Fresh air would be nice on my face.

The insides of my cheeks still tasted like scotch.

When Marie got to my apartment, we said good morning and hugged each other and then walked for quite a while without talking.

Finally, she said calmly, "How do you feel?"

She squeezed my hand in hers.

Marie has said that when I talk about my feelings it allows her to see that I am vulnerable and she likes that. But I've never considered vulnerability a strong asset.

"Mornings are so peaceful," I said.

She looked at me. Then she looked straight ahead again. "You seem distant."

"I'm okay."

"You sure?"

I didn't want to answer too fast, so I focused on walking. I let the weight of my whole body rest on each leg and foot before stepping forward. Since I wasn't feeling well, I was going slower than usual anyway, and the pace felt like a wise pace.

"Do you like being with me, Marie?"

"You know I do."

"I feel like you don't like the way I am sometimes."

Marie sighed. "We just don't see eye to eye on a lot of things."

"Like what?" I asked.

"You're carrying a container of salt, for one thing."

She had a point. I was. It had been on a curb in a pile of random stuff not too far from my apartment when we started out on our walk.

"So?"

"What're you going to do with it?"

"I'm taking it back to my place."

"For what?"

"It's just going to go to waste sitting back there. I need some anyway. Someone would've come by and thrown it out or knocked it over."

"Can I tell you something?" Marie dropped my hand and stopped walking. "When I watched you pick that up I thought to myself, 'He can't possibly eat that. There's no way.' But I didn't say anything because I know that's what you do. That's how you are choosing to live."

She paused. Then she grabbed my hand again.

"But I couldn't eat that."

"Sure you could," I said, holding up the paper cylinder.

The little girl on the side was wearing her yellow dress, walking in the rain. "It's just salt. It's fine."

"That's the point, though. I don't want to. I don't want to live like that."

"But you said you liked that I was resourceful and that I can do so much with so little."

"I know I did, but can you at least validate that I wouldn't do that? That I wouldn't eat food I found in the street?"

"What are we doing, then, you and me?"

"That's not what I mean."

"Then what *do* you mean?"

"I mean I have to start thinking about the future. You can get salt for two dollars, but you are going to use salt you found. Found salt. I love this about you, I really do, but you have to start taking better care of yourself. We have to think about where we're going."

I turned and looked down the street. The leaves had begun to change quickly now.

"I know where I'm going," I said. "And I *have* two dollars, I just don't want to spend it on salt. There are more pressing things I have to put my money toward. You know that. Crushing things. It's an awful weight."

The leaves rustled as we started walking again. "I hate being in this position," I said. "It feels ridiculous. And embarrassing. But I am, and I have to make sacrifices. If it makes you feel better, when I get home, if the salt seems bad or whatever, I won't use it."

"Jesus," Marie said softly, "it's not about the salt."

By then we had reached the park. I didn't know what else to say.

We headed for the swings. We sat in them and swung slowly in silence, but then I felt woozy, so I sat in the woodchips by the merry-go-round with my head between my knees.

"I think I better go," Marie said.

"Okay," I said.

I was uncomfortable sitting that way, so I tried crossing my legs, but then I immediately uncrossed them, stretching them out in front of me, and I leaned back on my arms. I thought I might throw up. My head was throbbing. I wanted to say something declarative, but I didn't know what that was.

I think Marie wanted me to say it, too. Instead of walking away, she stood looking at me. We were both waiting for me to say something confident and reassuring.

I leaned forward and grabbed my knees. Then I looked her in the eye. "What?"

"Nothing," she said. "I'll see you later."

I laid back on the playground. I stared up at the sky as it filled with sun for the day. The clouds were high and far apart. I could feel tiny pieces of wood stabbing into different parts of my back through my shirt, and through my hair into my head. It hurt slightly, but somehow took my mind off my skull, against which my brain was pounding in rhythm with my heart. *Thump, thump. Thump, thump. Thump, thump.*

I closed my eyes. I could hear the swoosh of blood moving near my ears and behind my temples. *Salt can't go bad, though,* I thought. *It's just a mineral.*

# 22

---

Hi. How's your Monday? Mine's okay. I'm on lunch out in front of the office and Michelle just walked by.

There aren't many trees where I work, which is unfortunate for a variety of reasons, but probably none so annoying as the fact that there's really nowhere I can eat without the sun beating in my eyes.

Michelle wore another floral print dress today. This time with a solid colored cardigan over the top because it's getting colder now.

"Wow," she said walking up. "Is that your lunch? What's all in there besides lettuce?" I was sitting and she was standing over me.

"Just lettuce, mainly," I said. "And some nuts." I looked into my reused bean dip container. "Almonds."

Most everyone in the office goes out to eat. I guess I

wouldn't mind doing that once in a while. But for now, because my resources are still scarce, I bring my own lunch and let them go without me. There are very few things to talk about in a group work setting anyway. And I don't usually like to talk about any of those things. Not weighing in on office drama makes me look like a jerk, though I'm not trying to be that. Besides, I like it in the sun, even if it's really bright.

"You're too funny, Nick."

But I didn't think the lettuce or I were very funny.

"We're going for pizza, if you want to come."

"That's okay," I said as kindly as I could. "Thanks, though."

"Why don't you ever come with us?"

I looked up and thought about telling Michelle the truth. "I guess I'm just trying to eat better and not spend too much money." Then I gestured with my fork toward the building. "I should be getting back anyway. Those checks aren't going to sort themselves."

"Suit yourself," Michelle said.

"Have fun," I said.

If I were her, I think I would have stopped asking me by now. But if she still asks when I get back on my feet, I'm going to go ahead and say yes once or twice. That would be a nice thing to do, I think.

I really should get back to work, but I want to sit here for a few more minutes and have a cigarette alone. The sun is having a soft moment. It's buttery in the fall. It comes down at a different angle in autumn than it does in summer, which really changes things.

Contrary to what I told Michelle, the checks do, sort of, organize themselves. What I do is receive and process people's payments to our small local company that builds and installs large industrial sinks. The actual industrial portion of Stevens' is in another part of the city. Our fifth floor office is just administrative. On each check that I receive there is a number and an invoice to which it corresponds. It's not like a check ever just comes in out of nowhere, someone giving us free money, so it's pretty easy to figure out what box you have to check in the spreadsheet to indicate to Greg that everything is on track and rightly balanced.

I just made smoke come out of the corner of my mouth. Sunlight is covering my face. When I look up and close my eyes, the backs of my eyelids are a warm orange instead of their usual black.

What I do at work is not very difficult. I'm pretty certain that any number of socialized primates or very smart fish could do it. That's probably why I'm not full-time, or compensated enough to pay off both my debt and my current bills and taxes in a timely and responsible fashion. That's also why I can't eat at restaurants very often. But it's the only job I can get right now, so I have to stick with it.

I wish I could tell you all about sinks, perhaps about

their amazing history, or the fact that sinks outsell all other major plumbing devices, even toilets. But I can't tell you those things, because all I do is process payments. I don't know any more about sinks than you do.

What I can tell you about is bicycles.

As a child I made a science fair project in which my Captain America action figure was on one end of a teeter-totter that I made from an old piece of cedar. On the other end sat Spider Man. I can't remember who was heavier, but I do remember sliding a small metal weight back and forth along the teeter-totter, close to and then away from the fulcrum, to demonstrate to the middle-aged judges walking around the gymnasium nodding and hmmming that I knew all about the "simple machine" known as "the lever." For my efforts, I received a participation ribbon. I still have it in a fireproof file box with my passport and various swimming lesson certificates and a letter I once wrote but never sent to Pope John Paul II, asking him what it was like to forgive his would-be assassin.

The fact that my bicycle is a simple machine pleases me, because if something goes wrong, I can probably fix it. There are really only a handful of parts that make up a bicycle.

This doesn't seem true, however, if you take a bicycle apart and lay all the pieces on the floor. All of a sudden, without you knowing it, there are thousands of confusing parts that look like they never once belonged on your bicycle, and yet here they are, spread out in your home with your greasy fingerprints all over them. It's confounding. But once you get them back together you think to yourself, *See, that wasn't so bad.*

And after you fix it yourself and take that bicycle for a spin around the block and then slowly start to ride it back and forth to work with a little regularity, it's something amazing that the world can't ever take away from you, because you did it with your own bare hands and your own true effort, making your own movement possible day after day after day.

My cigarette's out and my lettuce is all gone, so I'm going to head back in to work now.

# 23

I'm sorry to say that one of the cats shat on his hind legs this morning. I had to clean him up, which made me late to leave.

Maybe it was because I was later than usual, but the homeless man was livelier than normal when I went by. He was walking in small circles. It looked like a great debate was happening, but he was by himself.

"Hey," he said when he saw me. He smiled widely and his eyes seemed pried open. "That's a good bike."

I pulled over to the side of the road where he was walking around. "Yeah, I like it," I said.

"I'd rather smoke pot and take the bus myself."

"That's the safest way, probably," I said.

"Sitting there looking out the window. Just love it," he said, pulling his fists down from the sky. "Watching the world parade by." Then he made another little circle. When he looked back, I let him gaze off past me for a few seconds. Finally, he settled his look on my face.

"I've been meaning to give you this," I said. I reached into my pocket and handed him a five. "It's not much," I said, fumbling to put it squarely in his hand, "but it's for you."

We were quiet.

"Bless you," he said.

"Sure thing."

"Bless you," he said again.

"Take care, brother."

# 24

THIS MORNING was quite beautiful. I smelled fall floating in the air. It was like an invisible bouquet of pumpkins waved above the road. The wind was at my back, which it hardly ever is, a pumpkiny breeze blowing only as hard as I was riding. My legs churned without much concentration or effort—sheer equilibrium of movement.

I have taken two new steps each morning to ensure the peacefulness of my travel time. One, as I'm strapping my bag tightly over my shoulders, I chant softly to myself, *Zen champion, Zen champion*. It's an effort to calm down. And two, I have begun rolling my right pant leg up one more fold than the left, which means the left leg is at two full folds, the right leg at three.

There were a lot of riders at every point along my route today. When I rode by the homeless man, he was talking to someone else on a bicycle that I've never seen before. "The rain can go to hell," I overhead him say. "Doesn't do me any good to be rained on."

Then about halfway to work I remembered this is Ride Your Bike to Work Week. If you ride your bike to work every week, Ride Your Bike to Work Week is one of the worst weeks of the year. Ride Your Bike to Work Week sounds like a healthy, community-building concept. But unleashing into bike lanes and busy traffic hundreds of people who have not ridden a bicycle since early childhood isn't a very good idea, if you ask me.

Listen. Just this morning after I passed the homeless man, I saw these accidents waiting to happen:

+ a woman riding in a bushy coat with a furry hood over her eyes and a long cotton belt that dangled near her cranks

+ three different riders carrying heavy plastic grocery bags hanging off their handlebars

+ a man talking on a cell phone going downhill one-handed

I have never been rear ended by another bicyclist. But during Ride Your Bike to Work Week it almost happens every day.

When I got to work, I heard, "Hey, Nick."

It was Michelle.

"Can I ask you a question? It's about my bike."

This is another consequence of Ride Your Bike to Work

Week. Anyone who rides a bicycle on a regular basis becomes a prime target of questioning. "Hey, Nick, do you know why this part is stuck?" Or, "Nick, do you know what's making that noise?" And, "Hey, Nick, do you know what's wrong with my handlebars? They keep moving up and down like this."

The answer, 95% of the time, is simple: "Yes." Yes, I know why that part is stuck. And yes, I know what's making that noise. Yes, I can see what's wrong. What's wrong is that you do not ever ride your bike except during Ride Your Bike to Work Week.

Like anything else, bicycles need care and attention, but they rarely get any of that in the dark garage next to your son's old crib and the broken coffee table you've been meaning to take to the dump for years. There is a deep disrespect being shown to the bicycle when it's only ridden once a year and you have to ask someone else what's going on with it. It makes me cringe inside, as if a dead leaf were being crushed between my lungs. There is no dedication invested in these rides, no deep level of thought behind them. Everyone's just riding to fit in for a hot minute.

It's like some kind of office joke. Look at us! We're riding bikes, *to work!* If I drove a car and it was making a noise, would I come into the office and ask Michelle what was the matter? No, I wouldn't.

Wait.

*Zen champion, Zen champion.*

"Nick?" Michelle said.

She was standing next to her bike. On the downtube was a sticker that said, "TrailMaster." It was one of those hybrid deals with handlebars that come way up and a seat that's like a gel-filled pillowcase.

"Can I ask you a question about my bike?" she repeated. "I think that thing is getting hung up as I pedal." She pointed. "See?"

I didn't answer right away. I just looked at her bike, at the rusty chain and the frayed brake cables. Part of me wanted to tell Michelle that I could have a better look at lunch. Then I figured she might forget. It's not easy to remember to check on your bike during your break if you don't ever ride it. Things come up. People get busy. It's more convenient to put off pumping up your tires or tightening a few bolts. *I'll do it later*, you think, *as soon as I get home*. But at home there's mail to check and cats to feed and someone to call back. Doing things right away is the hardest way to do them. But if you don't, it catches up with you. Low tire pressure makes you prone to flats. Loose bolts breed other loose bolts. I know this from experience. Michelle doesn't respect her bicycle like she should, and I wanted her to know this and learn from it. I wanted her to see that riding to work isn't just some jokey thing to do.

But the morning was still beautiful and the sun was rising up over the buildings. I took a quiet, deep breath and looked at my hands. And then I said, "Which part?"

Michelle leaned down and pointed to her derailleur. “This one,” she said. She was wearing high heels and I was surprised her dress hadn’t become caught in her spokes on the way to work. She didn’t have a helmet, either. “See, it does this clicking thing.”

“I bet it’s a just little out of alignment. Here, let me have a look.”

“How do you know all this?”

“Lots and lots of practice,” I said.

I lifted up the back wheel and pedaled the bike with my hands. Sure enough, the chain was eddying between gears, making a grinding noise.

With the medium screwdriver from the tool bag in my backpack, I tinkered with the derailleur’s adjustment screws.

“Try that,” I said.

“Wow, thanks, Nick,” Michelle said, climbing on and circling the parking lot. “Yeah, the noise’s gone.”

“Thought so,” I said. “See you inside.”

“Okay!” Michelle hollered.

When I got to the door and looked back, she was still riding around in circles in the sun.

She didn’t see me see her. She was looking down, smiling.

# 25

Sometimes time just evaporates. Especially when the weather changes and I want to remain fully cognizant of what's occurring in the trees. At this time of year hillsides start to resemble elaborate model train sets.

It's lovely and manageable, this view of the city I have as I ride. The air wears a translucent cottony mask. Through it, evergreens become miniature replicas. Broad-leafed trees that have changed color stick out like painted plastic inserts. The houses are small and the cars all boxy, blues and yellows and reds.

As I pedaled by, the train went, *Whooot, whoooooooot*. It and the trees and the air are on a track headed elsewhere, into the dead of winter.

Over the train I watched the sun inch higher. Even as I witnessed it, I was convinced I was missing it all. I'm here, paying close attention, eyes wide open and staring, but it still happens too fast—so much faster than I'd like. Why can't it take longer, the amazing things, such as leaves falling into my path as I ride? Like weightless gold coins, they tumble back and forth, to and fro, down and down, and then somehow land right in my wire basket as I'm on the move. I'd like to stay in these moments. I want to see them all the way through until they're gone for sure. But they slip by before I can really get a good grasp on anything that's happening.

I should write this in my planner:

☒ Sunrise every day

and then make certain that I see the entire atmosphere tinting fuller and lighter, from total darkness until the sun is up completely. Then the sunrise will not have passed unnoticed.

On the corner by the train yard, three tall solitary trees stand in a line, planted along the sidewalk by the grocery store headquarters. Their trunks are whitish and today morning light bounced around in their orange tops. The experience of passing them was like riding my bicycle next to enormous blazing matchsticks. As if it's no big deal, here were these giant flaming matches burning as I pedaled myself to work.

The train again. *Whoot, whoot, whoooooooot.*

I had no idea where it was going, but I whispered to the huge machine, "Good luck."

Besides the matchstick trees and the leaves falling, there's other good news. In the last two months, I've never once forgotten to roll up my pants. No teeth marks whatsoever.

The bad news, though, is that Marie isn't talking to me. A few weeks ago we rode our bikes over to Christina and Abraham's house again. It was dark and raining heavily, which made it so my pants got wet all the way through to my underwear. I didn't really mind, because they would dry eventually, but it made Marie angry to get that wet, and it seemed like she was angry with me instead of at the rain. *It's just water*, I thought, but she wasn't of that opinion. On our way, a truck cut us off and yelled out the window that we should get a car.

Because they're nice folks, Christina and Abraham had the garage door open when we arrived and came out to meet us carrying steaming mugs of something.

"Wet ride, huh?" Christina asked, handing Marie a mug. "Hot toddies for you, then!"

Abraham gave me a hot drink and looked over my dripping bike. We all stood in the garage and sipped for a moment without talking. Abraham's pile of stuff was still over in the corner exactly as he'd left it.

"I've always liked your bike, Nick," he said. "Very classic."

"Thanks," I said. "Is it? Classic, I mean?"

"Well, yeah. That lugging is really gorgeous. Where'd you say you got it painted?"

"It came that way. Rides well, too, even on wet roads."

"And well lit, I see," he said.

"Yeah." I let the hot toddy course through every part of me. I felt at peace. The whisky in my bloodstream was making me forget how wet I was and how uncomfortable that ride had probably made Marie.

Then Abraham said, "Hey—where'd you get your light?"

I took another drink, pretending not to hear, letting the hotness pool in my empty stomach. "What's that?" I said.

"That bike light you've got there. I love those, even though they're kind of expensive. Where'd you get it?"

"Oh, the Knog?" I said. "I've had that one for a while. It's great having so many—"

"I have that one, too," he said, turning the light off for me. "It should be in the garage here somewhere. Let me look. I bet I can find it."

Marie was looking at me. Her makeup had smeared in the rain. I looked into my hot toddy.

"Jesus, Abraham, let them get inside, for God's sake," Christina said. "Look how wet they are."

"I don't see it," Abraham said. "I had it in this pile. It needed new batteries."

"Abraham," Christina replied. Then she looked at us. "Come on, you two. Let's get inside."

"You can have it if you want," I said to Abraham. "I have plenty."

"Naw, I don't need it. I'll find mine eventually. Things are a mess down here."

We went in. Christina had set out food, and over a couple hours we talked about several films I hadn't seen and some books I hadn't read. I tried to reference a few things that Michelle always talked about at work, like some funny Internet thing, but I could tell Marie wasn't having a good time. Maybe she wasn't having a good time because she could tell I wasn't having a good time.

It could have been a good time, but I just kept thinking about the matchstick trees and the fact that they will probably be less on fire tomorrow. Taking a picture of them would be a mistake, because then they would just look like trees next to the street instead of what they really are to me.

On the way home, Marie didn't say much. It had stopped raining, and was actually very pleasant. I wanted to stop somewhere and maybe see if the moon would come out. But we didn't stop at all, even for a minute.

"Thanks for inviting me," I said to Marie as we pedaled quietly along. We were on an unlit street and the moon cast a pale light. "It's nice to hang out with them."

"Are you serious?" she asked.

"Of course."

I was hoping we would ride to my apartment, but at

the turn we would take to get there, Marie turned right, toward her place. She didn't say anything, so I just rode behind her.

When we arrived, I made motions to lock up our bikes, like I do when I visit, both of them together in a knot in the backyard that no thief would dare untie, but Marie stopped me.

"Nick," she said, "I think you should go home."

"Why's that?" I said. "I thought you wanted me to come over."

"Let's not."

"Let's not what? Are you okay? Did I do something?"

"Do something? Well, let's see. Did you steal Abraham's bike light and put it on your bike and then have the audacity to ride over there with it and pretend you didn't?"

This was going poorly.

"Well, I guess I did that, yes."

"You took it," she said. "Goddamnit. I knew it as soon as he said it. Goddamnit, Nick. I mean, this is fucking crazy. You know that, right? The man I'm dating, a grown man, went into my friend's home and stole his bike light? Christ. What the hell were you doing? Why would you do that?"

"But—"

"Actually, I don't even want to know."

"He wasn't going to use it," I said. "It needed batteries, but he wasn't going to get around to it. It's been months since I took it and he didn't even notice. It would sit there forever. But I use it every day. That's worth something, isn't it?"

"No, it isn't."

"Wait."

"No. Go home. I'm not dealing with this."

"I'm sorry. I love you. That was stupid, even if I do use the bike light more than Abraham. I crossed the line. Out of bounds. I get it. That wasn't cool."

"Wasn't cool? What is this, junior high?" Marie put her face in her hands. "You can't just do shit like that because you think you would put some stupid light to better use. It's not your light. You don't get to do that. Life doesn't work that way. You need to figure some shit out."

"But it *should* work that way, shouldn't it?" I said. "It makes perfect sense."

"To *you*, Nick. It makes perfect sense *to you*. But that's not how things are. Bike lights get left in basements. People don't use every single last fucking thing they own. You can't go taking things just because you don't think they're being put to good use. Jesus fucking Christ," she said. Then she started crying. "I'm not going to do this," she said. "I'm just not."

Then she went inside and closed the door and left me in the yard.

I stood there a long time, just looking up at the night sky. The moon was breaking through. It was doing one of those famous Halloween tricks where it sits behind a wispy cloud and pushes its shrouded light out around the opaque edges. I wanted to ride under it for a long time, until it set or went behind other more dense clouds.

*Okay*, I said to myself. *This will be okay. I'll figure this out.*

I got on my bike and headed back to the intersection, and then turned the other way.

# 26

Hi again.

For lunch this afternoon I had:

+ cornbread

+ black beans

+ three crackers

+ and one hard-boiled egg

I also drank some water.

The cornbread would have tasted better had it not been moldy.

Today was one of my half days at Stevens', so after lunch I went on a long ride across the city to an antique shop. Bob's Antiques is owned and run by a man named Justin. You probably think the disconnect between language and reality bothers me, but I'm not letting it.

It's frightening to ride a bicycle in heavy traffic. For this reason I don't make a habit of cruising around town after work. But in this case I made an exception, because I have a plan.

I thought of this plan last night. In less than four months, barring a catastrophe, if I just keep doing what I have been doing and adhere to the repayment plan I've had for over three years, I'll be finished. Free and clear. Zeroed out. I won't owe anything to anyone. At that point the bulk of my paychecks won't go to paying off items I bought almost a decade ago, many of which I've since resold.

My plan, though, is to expedite the process. I'm going to sell an old wind-up gymnastics toy I found in my grandparents' estate many years ago. I wasn't sure why I kept it, but now it seems pretty clear: I held onto it in order to sell it at this exact moment—to put myself over the top. The box isn't in good shape, but the toy still works if you're gentle with it.

At work I ran a few Internet searches and found this same plastic pre-WWII Japanese contraption listed for close to $2000. If I had $2000, here's what I'd do: I'd put $1900 toward my debt, which would nearly round off this whole terrible process once and for all, and then I'd use $100 and take Marie out to dinner. There's a small restaurant she talks of often that she and I have never been to together: Cinelli's. I'd take her to Cinelli's. With $100 we could have a bottle of wine and large plates of pasta. We could laugh as the wine trickled through us and we could remark on how nice the weather was. We could drink the whole bottle and eat slowly and talk about how people don't read books anymore but that that's okay because books won't ever really die. Deep down, people like the way books feel in their hands. Books will always be around in some capacity, even if just as niche objects.

Then we could order tiramisu. Marie and I could sit back as the sun set and as people walked by on the sidewalk. We could watch them and speculate on where they're going and what they're saying and whether they'll end up buying any of the Things and Stuff in storefront windows across the street from the restaurant.

We could then, maybe over espresso, consider that if we got married, we wouldn't need very many Things and Stuff at all. In fact, we could probably fill a small house with items from Goodwill, or recycled objects, like a whole collection of glassware composed entirely of old peanut butter jars and olive containers and secondhand mugs that friends had given us. As we were wrapping up at the restaurant, I could explain that I'm just trying to make do without a few things during this rough patch and that being resourceful is one of the few things I can actually do well. It's the only weapon I have in a battle I've long been fighting.

"I'm so close to being done with this," I could say. "I promise. It's only going to get better." Then I'd pause. "Can you stick it out with me?"

Then we could lean across the table and kiss before I very gracefully paid the bill.

A meal experience like that could go a long way toward helping Marie forget that I picked up salt on the side of the road and took it home to use, and that I decided to repurpose Abraham's bike light and use it as my own.

I was thinking about all of this on my ride over to Bob's (Justin's). But as I approached that part of town, I decided that I'm not sure Marie would go for a house full of found items. If I'm honest with myself, which I need to be right now, Marie would probably not like having a house like the one I'm thinking of. I'd have to ask her what she wanted and see if I could live with that, too. And I think I could, if I tried.

A steel grate bridge spans the river before you get to the antique shop. If you go fast enough over something that is composed of slats, the slats sort of disappear. It's a complicated optical experience involving perspective and speed and geometry. Wheels do this in car commercials. It looks like the wheel is barely moving at all, or if so, only slightly, and not in sync with how fast the car is going, or even in the right direction. Sometimes it even looks like the wheel is moving backward, though the car is going forward. Propellers play this trick, too, and regular old ceiling fans. Like those things, the slats on the bridge fell into a rhythm as I was riding over them. Looking down, I saw a pattern of the whole, instead of all the individual parts that made it up. But it's important to remember that there are many tiny slats that get you from one side of the bridge to the other. Riding quickly I could look down through the nonexistent slats to the water below, and I felt like I was flying.

But when I arrived at the antique store, Justin wasn't in. "Oh, Justin's gone for the afternoon," the dark haired woman behind the counter explained.

"This morning when I called, he said he'd be here till five."

"No, he's off already."

The ride had taken me 55 minutes. So would the ride home.

"Okay," I said. I held the toy in my hand. "Maybe I'll try later in the week."

On the way home, on the steel grate bridge, I rode as slowly as possible so that I could see and feel every slat I went over.

# 27

I'm HAVING another cigarette this morning out on the porch. I just tried to let it dangle from my lip like a cowboy might.

I am very tired.

I'm not making enough changes. It would be easier to start with the stuff that I'm not very convinced of or all that into, like smoking. So I'm quitting. Right after this, I'm not going to smoke anymore.

Perhaps smoking is what's wrong with my energy level. Problem is, this morning I have been thinking more about communing with other people who smoke, especially people who used to smoke but have since passed away, as in historically. I recognize, like you, that smoking is bad for me and that Marie probably doesn't like it and perhaps still isn't talking to me because I do things like smoke. So I think I'm going to stop.

But then again there were thoughtful and effective politicians in the 1930s and 40s who had to make important decisions that would affect many millions of people. They smoked. They would lock themselves in their secret governmental rooms in Washington and light up and hash out together what they had to do. They would drag so deeply on their cigarettes that their heads would tilt back smoothly. In times of crisis, they would seal the smoke off in their lungs while they thought, and then would exhale a beautiful translucent *V* on which would be carried the answer to the nation's problem. I wish I could sit in one of those rooms right now and have a cigarette, too, just to watch how they handled the pressures of having to do something that someone else will notice.

I like that our current President is a smoker. In fact, since I've been smoking, I'm convinced all Presidents should be smokers.

One of my favorite visions of bicycling is of those men who would race the nascent Tours de France over mountains and cobblestones with cigarettes hanging out of their mouths. I'm sure you've seen the image, the one where the guy is riding without hands and his teammate to his right is steadying him by holding his shoulder and the teammate to his left is lighting his cigarette for him while also riding with no hands. It's a famous picture. But I like the guy in back. He's there in the middle, right in the midst of the action, but in the background and hardly noticeable because the better and more photogenic of his cycling buddies are taking up the foreground of the frame. But he's there nonetheless, probably doing his difficult thankless job as a *domestique*, with his hand raised in exaltation, a smile on his wide face.

The riders used to believe smoking would increase their lung capacity before and during a race, which seems like a silly thing to think. Then again, smoking makes me feel pretty powerful, even if my energy's lower, so I get where they were coming from. With a cigarette and the right combination of words and listeners, I could explain what I'm thinking so articulately that whole communities would be moved to ride bicycles to work and spend only cash, because bicycles and cash are real things that you can feel and see and that affect you when you use them. Not like cars and credit cards.

What I need to do is get down to business and clear out what I'm not using and pay some of these bills. That would definitely be a place to start. Now that I've stopped smoking as of this morning, after this cigarette, it's time to take on other important tasks that are going to make a difference in the long run. For example, I've made these decisions in just the last few weeks:

+ I've started going without underwear instead of wearing ratty ones. Having holey underwear is a bad sign, so I threw them all away. Now I don't wear underwear, but I would at some point in the near future like to get some new pairs.

+ I feel like I'm discounted by other bicyclists because

of the socks I wear. But I'm going to keep wearing them anyway, because I like the way they look. At least they don't have holes.

+ I am going to make myself bread to eat once a week. I really am in awe of bread, how it rises there in the oven, up out of the pan and into this little mound of tastiness. Brilliant. Just brilliant.

+ On a postcard to my friend Andrew, I asked if he'd be willing to design and build a coffin out of plain pine that I could buy from him and save for when the day comes. He is a great woodworker and I'd rather have the money for that expense go to someone I know and respect than some business I'd never been to before I died. Plus, then no one would have to deal with that purchase later on. I'll already have taken care of it.

+ The water bill is due tomorrow, but instead of riding around the park thinking about what to do, I sold 32 books and my hiking boots yesterday. After that, without thinking too much about it, I rode the cash to the bank and deposited it. Then I wrote a check for the whole balance, sealed it up in the envelope provided, rode it over to the bureau's drop box, and let it go into the metal mouth of the receptacle.

One thing I didn't do was go back to Bob's Antiques. That may not have been the best plan after all. I've thought of something better.

My last cigarette just burned out. Time to go to work.

# 28

THERE IS a post office in my neighborhood that I like to visit because the man who works there obviously exercises on a regular basis. In my mind I've nicknamed him Strong Arms.

Whether he knows it or not, Strong Arms is an inspiration. He wears a standard issue USPS polo shirt, as he has to, but given this limited wardrobe selection, he's chosen the size of his free employee uniform carefully: not too baggy and not too tight. His arms don't so much bulge out of this shirt as they come right up to the circumference of the sleeve cuffs in a very natural fashion. His arms discretely announce that, yes, he's been working out these past few years, and yes, he's made some good decisions. With his spare time, rather than, say, watch television, drink whisky, or go on dates, Strong Arms has exercised so that he fits into a size large collared t-shirt perfectly. He makes me want to do the same.

The post office is in general a place of great angst. There never seem to be enough employees to serve the stream of customers. I visit Strong Arms's post office because it's tucked away over in my neighborhood. It's a short ride and less crowded. There's a blackberry thicket on the way growing up along the rail yard, to boot. To eat a blackberry straight from the bush in the middle of the city can make you forget altogether the other things you're looking for.

Strong Arms is the only employee I've ever seen at this hidden postal branch. As I watch him help each person in line, I can tell he has stopped on many occasions to think about what he's doing. With his life, I mean. You can see it in how he moves behind the counter with practiced poise. His voice is calm and slow and disarming, even when he's outnumbered almost ten to one. I've never seen him flustered or even slightly frazzled. Even-keeled Strong Arms. I envy his composure.

Anyway, I rode there this evening before it closed at six. My bike basket was piled high with packages. Eight, to be exact. Sealed and addressed to eight people who had purchased books of mine online. If you order a book from me, I mail it to you as soon as I possibly can. I want to keep a "starred profile" so that the books on my shelves keep selling. The thing that's often overlooked when you sell a book online is that your customer doesn't know anything about you whatsoever, except two things: 1) when their book arrives, and 2) what condition it's in. Otherwise, they don't care for you at all, which is fair enough.

On my way to the post office, though, I had an accident.

I don't usually leave with anything in my basket that's not securely strapped down. What would happen to the contents of my basket if an earthquake struck? Nothing. It's strapped that well.

But today I made an exception. $119 worth of book sales in my basket, unstrapped. They fit well enough and didn't look like they'd wiggle around as I rode, so I didn't bother. But as I was rounding the last curve to the post office, right after you come up a little hill and pass the Scottish store, I cut my right turn too tight for the amount of weight I had on the front and

— *WHAM!* —

I wrecked right off the front of my bike. Books went everywhere on the moist blacktop. I only wanted to ride my bike and sell some books and maybe chat with Strong Arms, and yet here I was on the ground surrounded by bruised parcels. Worst part is, the recipients would wonder why their books were dirty. If I wasn't before, I'm now wholly convinced "exception" is synonymous with "mistake."

But I tried to pull myself together. *No problem*, I thought.

I brushed off my pants and then picked up the books, all wrapped in reused paper bags and heavily taped. Once I made it to the front of the line, Strong Arms accepted each of the packages at media rates. He didn't even ask why the packages were wet.

I didn't feel like riding home, so I walked beside my bike instead. It didn't start raining, but it smelled like it might. There weren't any trees to look at, but I did see a cat sitting on a fence.

As I walked, I thought a lot about gravity and how much everything weighs. Then I thought about the short Stephen Crane poem that goes: "A man said to the universe: / 'Sir, I exist!' / 'However,' replied the universe, / 'The fact has not created in me / A sense of obligation'."

Further along, I was nearly knocked to the ground again when I saw this:

It was graffitied on the wall under the overpass not far from my apartment.

# 29

---

Tonight, after I wrecked, I decided to take a bath.

Steam rose off the exposed parts of my naked body as I sipped some Mr. Walker. Due to the laws of displacement, I could set my small glass of whisky right in the water and it would float around next to me, which was fascinating. It started out to my right, sailing around that part of the tub, but after I took another sip and set it back on course, it careened around the cape of my raised knee and moved slowly back up to the northern hemisphere of my chest.

My little boat of whisky. It was on a journey, a trip it didn't even know it was going to be launched on five minutes ago. At any moment, if I moved too hastily beneath the surface like some human bathtub Kraken, it might capsize, sink, and clink down on the porcelain bottom with a soft metallic noise, giving up its alcoholic content to the bathwater that rushed over its sides when I shifted.

The bathroom was cold but my legs and arms were hot, even though they weren't underwater. I stared up at the tiles rising above the tub on three sides, interlacing black and white, black and white, black and white, and let myself stay in the stare for as long as it would last. Wisps of steam kept rising off my fingers into my line of vision. Then I started focusing intently on the showerhead without blinking—on its little concentric circle of spouts, like the holes of a bicycle wheel, and the spokes of water it was capable of raining down. The longer and more keenly I stared—now its holes reminded me more of a hub than a wheel, since these were holes in close proximity, a hub that was far away and spinning off into the distance—the fuzzier it became. Why does such hard focus produce the opposite effect, like when you look at stars?

I finally broke the stare and looked slowly around the rest of the tub. I was out of soap, because when it gets to be a small sliver I put it in my shampoo bottle. That way, no part of the soap ever goes to waste. I save the tiny soap shards from falling down the drain. Then I force them into the top of the container. I figure the solid soap will dissolve among the liquid shampoo and I'll have made the most of both.

I once showered with a canteen and a rock. I was camping, and it was all that was available for getting clean, but that may have been the cleanest I've ever been. I wonder if there is a way to live like I'm camping, but still be in a house in the city? I don't mean like sitting around a campfire in the backyard. I mean living so that everything I have could fit in my backpack. I mean being able to know exactly what's in my bag without ever looking. Knowing that beside the toilet paper is a small trowel in the outside uppermost pocket. Or that my raingear is on top of the medical kit on top of the food at the top of the bag. Or that my six t-shirts are in a Ziploc on the bottom near the stove and the fuel and the water purifier, which are next to another Ziploc of argyle wool socks along with their matching polypropylenes. I wouldn't even need to carry soap, because a young river rock on dirty skin with frigid stream water from a canteen is one of the best showers in the world.

Both of the cats came into the bathroom and sat down next to each other on the towel beside the tub and looked at me for a long time. I reached out and petted each of them with my wet hand, a gesture that didn't even make them flinch. I thought cats disliked water, but not my cats. These cats don't give water a second thought. They watched with big eyes as I sipped again from my whisky skiff. In the eyes of the tallest cat, I could see myself. The light was low, and so his pupils were those enormous full-eye pupils cats get when they are hunting, and there I was, naked and looking back at my own reflection, sitting in the bath with one arm over the side and mouth ajar.

Though the water didn't faze him, the tall cat didn't look

happy, either, nor did he seem to be enjoying the fact that he was here. Rather than sitting on my lap in the chair in the living room like he would prefer, he was watching me drink whisky from a small glass that floated around the bath.

I wish it were feasible to sit in the bath for an entire year and grow out my beard and let everything go on without me. What would it take to have a full beard, one that puts people off and makes it so that they wouldn't ask me any questions about my bike, because there was so much hair around my mouth and nose? As of this week, I have let my beard grow longer than I ever have, and I often wonder how long it would take to get it three dimensionally magnificent. Short on the sides, but full and round off my chin, making a tight, interlaced bundle of hair—a Melville type of beard. I haven't in the past had patience or incentive enough to see how long it could possibly grow. So I thought about it for a long while, the length and aspirations of my beard, sitting there in the tub, touching my chin and cheeks with my free wet hand. *I'm just going to go ahead and relax here for a while and let this thing grow on*, I thought.

After I don't know how long, I started to prune. When I finally sat up, preparing to get out of the tub, water slid from my skin like a thick cloak. I pulled my hands up from the tub bottom where they had been resting, and where the blood in my arms had settled to the streambeds of my veins. Very slowly, so that I could really sense the fact that I was rising up out of the bath into the cold air, I moved my hands up through the bathwater as gradually as I could. When they had broken the surface—very slowly, like two wrecked ships being hauled up from the ocean floor—I put them on the sides of the tub and lifted myself out of the water for good. I had set a course before me and could see it clearly now. Blood rushed through my body. I could feel it moving in me, through my neck and legs and eyes. The sound of it was loud in my ears, a windy pulsing noise.

Sometime later, I woke up on the bathroom floor to the smaller cat licking drips of water off my legs. I felt dizzy, but not uncomfortable. I possessed no desire whatsoever to move my limbs or head. I just laid there in the cloudiness. The linoleum was cool on my face and I wondered if I could just sleep through the night. The bristly buds of the cat's tongue felt sharp on my skin.

It will not surprise you that while lying naked on the bathroom floor, I dreamed of riding a bicycle. Many parts of dreams don't make any sense, but a few facets of this one matched up pretty well with my real life. For example, my dream didn't feature any sci-fi or pornographic situations. It was just me riding my same green bike that I ride everyday. As I was riding, I had to be pedaling, which is pretty much the same as it is when I'm going to work, though I suppose I could lift my feet off my pedals and just let them spin for the fun of it, which I've done once or twice before. What I did in the dream, though, was sit upright in the saddle and ride astutely. I rode around for a long time looking at a lot of very beautiful scenes. I saw the matchstick trees again, when they were still aflame, and I noticed I was wearing an entirely argyle suit that had a hole in one elbow. *I'll have to patch that*, I thought. Soft banjo music played in the background somewhere. Little puffs of smoke came up from the brick chimneys of houses around me like perfect tiny pipe cleaners. At one point on the ride, I passed by Marie's house and she was out front on her patio, eating an apple, but I couldn't stop pedaling, so I waved. I motioned down to my fast moving pedals.

"Can't stop!" I yelled.

"I know!" she said. "Be safe!"

"Here I go, then!" I hollered, and rode on by her house, looking over my shoulder, still waving.

At a large hill I stood on the cranks and rode with ease up the long incline. My unbuttoned argyle suit coat blew horizontally behind me. "I am the one," I said under my breath. "I can tell by the way I'm riding. I've never seen anyone ride up this hill at such a speed. I shouldn't be able to ride so fast."

Crowds of onlookers suddenly lined the road as I went on. "It's him," they murmured. "He's the one."

At the hill's apex, though, I realized there was a blockade

of dump trucks coming my direction. But I just kept pedaling. I had to. It was a fixed gear. Right before I met the dump trucks head on, at top speed, I put the bike down on its left side and slid. I don't know what I thought I was doing. Why would I do that? Why would I try to slide underneath a phalanx of dump trucks rather than swerve out of their way, or get off the bike and hold up my hand and convince them to stop driving? Not me. I wrecked right into them. The skid ripped my argyle pants and gave me an instant rash all over my legs and hip.

The crowd went quiet, and then everyone dispersed, heads lowered. Even the dump trucks left. They just reversed and went back to wherever they had come from.

# 30

At some point I must have made it to my bed. I was lying there uncomfortably, squinting against the pallid early winter light coming through the blinds. It was as though, like gilded gold, the sunlight had been beaten thin and stretched to fill the sky. That beating went on, too, in the back of my head. The whisky. Everything was being slowly pounded out, like a building drawing nearer to completion, brick by brick. The mallet strokes were so loud I closed my eyes again.

I couldn't stop thinking about Marie. I just laid there, wondering if she missed me. I tried to remember what her breasts looked like. I also thought about her teeth. Then I wondered if I shouldn't have just left the light on the floor and the salt on the curb and never mentioned anything about the way she locks a bicycle.

I had my eyes closed, trying to fall back asleep. Maybe I could have a different dream in which I didn't wreck and instead just kept pedaling right into the parked trucks, as fast as I could. You can't look away forever, though, so I finally peeked, easing the morning into focus. Through the fuzzy slits of my eyelids I watched dust particles climb a ladder of pale sunbeams. *There they go*, I thought. *Out of the house and into the world. Carried away by the changing wind.* I supposed that was their job.

The tall cat was lying on my chest, legs pulled beneath his body, staring at me.

"What?" I asked him.

He blinked slowly.

"I know."

The white and gray fur of his nose and mouth was short, but his whiskers were unwieldy things, easily three and a half inches long. I knew right then that I'd never have a Melville beard.

In the kitchen I made a pot of coffee. While it brewed, I sat at the table, putting both hands down on its cold surface. I spread my fingers out. The room filled with the smell of brewing coffee. I looked at my hands, then turned them over, looking at the creases in my palms. These hands had not made anything. They had not built a home, or a piece of furniture, or even so much as a derby car since I was just a boy. And yet the creases were deep, as though I had at one time made a grand thing that still stood somewhere. Then I made two fists. I clenched them hard once or twice, and then held them in a tight ball until I couldn't hold them anymore.

The coffee finished and I poured myself a mug. Just black, without any milk or honey. Remember how I said I had a better plan than Bob's Antiques? Well, I do. I've put my mind to it and I think it's going to work.

I'm going to buy a car.

Then I can take Marie to the beach, just like she wanted. On our way, I'm going to tell her how I sat in my kitchen and drank coffee and made this decision. I'm going to tell her it's important for me to winnow down the books I own so that I'm an authentic representation of myself. Then I'll explain that I want to be next to her for as many nights as possible. "The Nick you see before you now," I'll say in the car on the way to the coast, "is only a cocoon, a knitted cotton shell of a man out of which the truly confident and balanced Nick, the real Nick, the one I've long envisioned and strived so long to become, is about to be born." *Nicholas*, with strong arms, his obstacles overcome.

There I'll be, driving us along.

By the time I was done with my coffee, the sun was on the floor and starting to spread its way up the wall.

# 31

---

JUST LIKE THAT, the matchstick trees are bare, fully burned up for the winter.

Now there was nothing left for me to look at on those branches as I leaned into the first corner on my way to work. Nothing but a wooden skeleton. I could see grey sky through the limbs. I could also see my own small billows of breath. Some people like winter, but I'm not one of them. It's too dark for too long.

My ride was lonelier without the trees. The homeless man was also gone. I wondered where he went.

Since the trees were done, here's what I thought about instead:

+ ancient marble statues

+ whether I have a nemesis

+ what Marie's been up to

+ sailing merchant ships
+ truth and justice
+ small loaves of bread

The ride was cold, but I didn't wear a coat. I wanted to feel the frigid breeze pierce my shirt and chill my moving body. I don't know why, but my legs felt strong in the sheathes of my pants, as though they fit in them just right. The movement, the *shush-SHUSH, shush-SHUSH, shush-SHUSH* of my pedaling up and down, pumped blood to parts of my body I swear I hadn't felt in years.

# 32

I HAD MY hands cupped over my eyebrows as I pressed my face against the driver's side window of a used brown sedan. The seats were faded and the roof liner had been removed or ripped out, leaving tawny metal exposed on the ceiling of the car. I stepped back to have a look at the tires, like I thought I should. Was I supposed to kick them?

Out of the corner of my eye I saw a salesman in a suit jacket and jeans coming toward me with his arm raised. His coat wasn't buttoned, so it sort of flapped behind him as he walked. His jeans gathered down around his shoes where they would without question get caught straight away in the chain of a bicycle.

"Great day, isn't it?" he called out as he waddled in my direction. He tugged at his belt loops to straighten up his pants and get them back to riding where I imagined they had been for only few moments very early in the day. The colorful tie that swayed back and forth across his stomach hypnotized me. I grew nervous watching it bend over the convex curve of his midsection. The salesman's belt made an arc as it came from his hips where the two ends dipped below his belly and just barely met at a stressed buckle. *What am I doing?* I wondered. And for about the tenth time since I walked onto the lot, in order to remain calm and undaunted, I reminded myself: *Marie. You're doing this for Marie.*

From the small building in the middle of the lot, a few lines of used cars radiated out in every direction, none of the cars much different from the one into which I was now staring. Sunlight caught the cars' windshields, and when I looked back to this large and smiling man, their paint jobs reflected small bright swirls into my eyes.

"What can I do you for?" he said at the same loud volume he had used from across the lot.

"Just sort of browsing right now," I said, trying to avoid the sun. Despite rehearsing how this would go, I was still nervous, and was afraid he'd hear it in my voice. "But I'm interested in a car."

Several of the more aerodynamic models at the dealership were parked on large swatches of carpet inside the building. Past the man, I could see a couple making slow circles around a low-to-the-ground convertible. They pointed every once in a while at different sections of the vehicle. The man, standing a few feet back, had his arms crossed, and the woman would go up intermittently and touch whichever part of the car she was talking about, massaging the rounded auto body as she looked at the man.

"This one gets great gas mileage," said the salesman, slightly out of breath and leaning on the car's side mirror. "Plenty of safety features. You're looking for something used?"

"Well, I don't necessarily have a lot to work with, so I just wanted to get a sense of what's available."

"Sure, sure," he said. "That's no problem."

"What isn't?"

"Take a look at the trunk here. Tons of room. You enjoy the outdoors? You look like a sporty guy."

"Biking," I said. "I ride quite a bit."

"Sure. Look at this thing. Opens right up. You could fit a bike in there, don't you think? Just lay it on its side."

"Maybe," I said.

"What's your budget?" he asked.

"Pretty low," I said.

"You're going to have to do a little better than that. What are we talking here? Young guy like you. Five or six thousand?"

"The sticker says three, but I could probably meet you in the middle."

The salesman hiked his pants up again. "Doesn't quite

work like that. Did you have a look at the nice little truck I've got over yonder? The white one? That one's down around 2K."

"I'm not much into trucks, really."

"You're not, huh?"

"I just want something I can take to the beach, maybe for some car camping."

"Goin' on a road trip?"

"You could say that," I said. He was pausing after everything I said now, as though maybe something was wrong, but I tried to stay calm and focused.

"You'll be puttin' a lot of miles on it, then."

"I'm not going across the country, if that's what you mean. Just to the coast."

He looked back at the small building and then up at the sun, head tilting far enough back for a second that I could see thick hairs on his neck that he had missed shaving. "You buyin' a car for just one trip?"

Now I was really flustered. I took my hands out of my pockets and then immediately put them back in again.

Then he said, "No matter. A truck'll get you there just the same. You can put your lawn chairs and firewood back there without worrying about the upholstery."

"A car would be smarter, though, wouldn't it? In case it rains, or if there's more than one person with me?" I asked, trying to assert myself. At work I had read up online about negotiation tactics, and I wanted to stay firm to look in control. *I'm buying a car from you*, I said to myself. *I'm running this transaction.*

"Walk with me," he said.

We crossed the lot, passing a host of vehicles of several makes and sizes, almost 100% of which were out of my price range. Actually, every car on this lot was out of my price range. I was in no position whatsoever to start making payments on a motor vehicle. Zero. That was my budget. Did he have that? A free car that I could drive over to a woman's house to show her that I'd done it, that I'd figured it all out and I was ready to go on outings like she and I had talked about? *Here's relatively reliable transportation that we can take camping next weekend if you'd like. Would you like that? To go with me? I have a tent and a camp stove. When you were talking about getting a car yourself you said we could make a trip to the coast. I can roll up my pants a bit farther than usual and as soon as we pull up I can hop out of the car and run toward the waterline and wade out and then run down the beach like a sprinter. You'll see that I'm kind of athletic and can move with a svelteness you didn't notice in me before. You always thought I was a tad pudgy, but now, watching me stride down through the water, splashing with each step, you'll see that maybe you were wrong, or that at least I've lost a little weight, because I have. It's all the bike riding, but now, with a car again and this plan, you'll see I'm not so bad. Peculiar, for sure, but who isn't? We'll build a fire, have a few drinks, then doze off with our heads peeking just a bit out of the open tent as we watch the stars fade into view. Lovely. It will be completely lovely.*

"Can't get much for fifteen hundred bucks nowadays," the salesman said as we approached the truck. To the left of it was a maroon Mitsubishi almost identical to the one I had once owned and sold. I wondered for a second if it wasn't actually the very same car. I tried to look at the hood and see if there was a small chip out of the paint where a rock had flown up when I was on the highway, but I didn't see anything.

"What do you need a car for anyway?" the salesman asked.

"It's a long way to the ocean."

"You don't have a car now?"

"Not for a couple years."

"You've been pedaling the bike around that long, huh?"

"It's not so bad."

We walked around the modest Toyota truck. "Have a look. You got your bike you can throw right in here like this," he said, making a swinging motion with his arms as though he was tossing a giant bag of soggy leaves into the bed with ease, "and then you and whoever else hop in and head off to where you're going, the beach or whatever. This thing'll drive over sand far better than that four-door you were looking at."

"I don't think I'm going to be doing any off-roading."

"I'm just saying you never know. Here, get in." He unlocked the driver's side and then went around to the passenger's side. "I'll assume you're licensed?"

"Of course," I said.

"Like I said, you never know. What's your name?"

"Nick," I said.

"Tom," he said, reaching across the cab of the truck to shake my hand.

"Nice to meet you, Tom," I said.

Once we were off the lot and settled into traffic, Tom said, "You can speed up more than that."

"I'm just not used to driving, that's all."

"Sure," he said.

I drove a few blocks. We didn't say anything, so I pretended to look diligently at all the dashboard lights and listen intently to the engine. Tom said, "Hey, what's a man like you doing buying a truck like this, anyway? It's hard to believe you're looking at something so economical."

"What do you mean?" I asked. Now I was really convinced something was wrong and that I'd ruined my chances to get to the ocean.

"Had a car, then you didn't, now you want another one—but you're only interested in the lowest end of the market?" Tom said. "Watch your speed in this section here. Cops are always giving tickets to people who are on test drives."

I was going to see if I could get out of answering Tom's question, but he seemed like one of those guys, an arm-wrestler or a veteran, who could wait you out no matter what was on the line. So I said, "Credit card debt. Got in over my head."

"Shit. It had to be more than that if you've been pedaling that bike around the city everyday."

"Not when you don't take care of it, it doesn't. $35,000."

"Okay. That's impressive. Take a right at this light," Tom said. "But you messed up, is all. Nothing wrong with that."

"But you've got to pay it back if you do."

"Did you declare bankruptcy?"

"What, and pass the problem on to someone else? It isn't anyone else's responsibility."

"So you paid back $35,000?"

"Most of it," I said. "And I'll be done soon."

Back at the lot, Tom had me park in front of the little building. We walked in. The couple was gone, but the convertible was still on its carpet in the middle of the room.

"Well, whaddaya think?" Tom said, sauntering back to a cubicle in the corner.

"I like it," I said. "I think it's what I'm looking for."

"You sure? I thought you didn't like trucks," Tom asked. "Maybe you want to save up, then come back and talk."

"Yeah," I said. "Pretty sure. What's it going to hurt to run the numbers?"

"All right. Have a seat for a minute and fill this out." He slid a clipboard across the small desk to me. "Coffee or anything?"

"I'm okay, thanks."

Tom left me with the clipboard and a pen. His desk seemed messy even though there wasn't much on it besides a desktop calendar, a computer, and a small photocopy tacked to the side of the cubicle: that image of a kitten dangling on a tree branch. *Hang in there!*

A different couple was looking at the convertible now, walking in the same slow circles, leaning in close to each other every once in a while to whisper.

I filled out the form.

"Well, what do we have?" Tom said, sitting down at the desk and taking a bite of bagel. Without waiting for an answer, he took the form from me and started punching away at his keyboard. After only a few seconds he said, "Interesting."

"What's interesting?"

He kept looking at the screen and mumbling and nodding his head. "Actually, everything looks fine. We can do 4.9% APR and zero down."

"Really?" I said. "That's excellent. I thought my credit was terrible."

"That's not what I'm getting. When was the last time you ran a credit check? I mean, your score's not outstanding, but I could have gotten you into a car twice this price. Lots of people have it way worse."

I looked out the window at the pick up. If it didn't rain, I figured everything would fit in the back perfectly.

"Looks like you have yourself a new truck," Tom said.

# 33

I WAS GOING to wait, but it was Saturday, so I drove to Marie's house directly from the dealer. When I arrived, I wanted to pull into the driveway, but there was already a car there, so I settled for a spot on the street. I went slowly up the walkway to the porch, standing straight. I didn't want to seem like I was hurried.

Marie pulled the front door open. "What's going on?" she said. She stood behind the screen door, which was still closed. Through it I could make out the silhouette of someone sitting in the living room. "What are you doing?" she asked.

"Can I come in?" I said.

"Now's not a very good time."

"I just wanted to ask you a question."

"What is it?"

"I wanted to know if you would like to go to the ocean tonight."

"What're you talking about?"

"You said you wanted to go to the ocean, and as of today, I can get us there." I stepped to the side and gestured with my hand toward my new truck.

"Whose is that?" Marie said.

"It's mine. I bought it this afternoon."

A man's voice came over Marie's shoulder. "Is everything all right?"

"It's fine. I'll be back in a sec," she said, stepping out of the house and shutting both doors behind her.

"I didn't know you had company," I said. "Sorry about that. I can get going."

Marie pulled her sweater around her waist and sighed. Her ponytail was coming loose. Strands of hair came down around her face. "Did you really buy that truck?"

"Yeah."

We glanced at it together. I thought she was going to cry again.

"Can you afford that?" she asked.

"I don't know," I said. "I don't think so."

"Why'd you buy it, then?"

"The ocean."

"Nick." She paused, shaking her head. "I don't think I'm in love with you."

"Is that who's inside?"

"Which means you can't drop by unannounced." She

ran her hands over her eyes like she was washing her face, then tucked her hair behind her ears. It looked like she was shivering. "And you can't go buying trucks."

"Tom said it's a solid truck."

"Tom?"

"The salesman."

"It's the beginning of winter."

"But I thought this is what you wanted. To go to the ocean."

Marie put her hands deep in the pockets of her sweater and shrugged. "Things change. People move on."

"I was going to build a campfire."

She looked me in the eye then, and I looked back. I stood as tall as I could, making sure I wasn't slouching.

"I have to get back inside," she said.

The door closed. I looked at the screen and the wood and the brass knocker for a few seconds. Then I turned around and just stood there on the porch. I put my arms to my sides and let my shoulders fall.

For a minute I looked out at the yard and the slim slice of the world that I could see from there. I studied the car in the driveway, an attractive German thing recently washed and waxed. It looked fast and comfortable to drive. The trees were bare, the sun was close to setting, and I felt cold for the first time. Smoke was coming out of the chimney next door and it smelled like pine everywhere. As slowly as I'd come up the walk, I strolled back to the truck.

# 34

I HAD the window down. Cold air came in at me so fast it made my eyes water. On the highway I couldn't tell one tree from another. It was a blur of green, the sky a smear of gray.

I'd grabbed an old sleeping bag from my apartment. It was a green quilted mummy bag. Little puffs of goose feathers came out when I rolled it up and tied it with the ties sewn into the bottom of the bag. My dad gave it to me at some point after my mom died, when he was starting to clean up and get rid of things to keep busy and not think too much about everything that happened.

I also had my filed credit card statements with me. Folders and folders full of them. And what was left of the Johnnie Walker. And a grocery bag filled with old newspapers, and a book I hadn't read that I pulled from my shelf. I had all of that in the truck's cab.

The road to the beach is flat for a while, before it goes over small mountains of evergreens and drops down to the sea. This is where the clouds get trapped in stands of tall spruces like the cotton balls kids glue on their drawings.

I was getting my first real look inside the truck, so I leaned over and opened the glove box as I drove. It was still full of papers from the previous owner. I pulled everything out and put it on the seat beside me. This is what was there:

+ an old parking ticket
+ handwritten notes, scrawled on top of other notes
+ two matchbox cars
+ a little leather folder
+ an unused condom

The breeze from the window shuffled the papers and tossed a few to the floorboard. Among everything else was a $20 bill, like money left in a coat pocket between seasons.

I drove along the coast and picked a campground on the cape that said it was open year-round. There wasn't a campground host or anyone at the entrance station, so I took the site closest to the sea. I wondered if I should pay, but decided not to care. As far as I could tell, no one else was there.

I backed the truck onto a slab of concrete. A wooden picnic table sat squarely on some bluegrass with a fire ring next to it. The site was surrounded on three sides by willow bushes. A faint path led into them. On the other side I could hear the ocean landing on the beach, but I didn't feel like walking down to it.

It was pretty dark by then, so I turned on the truck's headlights and scrounged around in the bushes for some kindling. I built a small teepee of sticks over a dozen balls of newspaper. Once I got the fire going I looked around for bigger logs. Someone in the adjacent site had left a few—enough to burn the remainder of the night. The logs were wet, and smoked heavily when I put them over the burning sticks. In time, they would dry and burn just fine. It wasn't raining, but seemed like it just had, and I figured it would again soon.

I pulled out the Johnnie Walker and the manila folders and set them all on the picnic table and sat down. I'd forgotten a mug, so I sipped directly from the bottle. No one else was there, but I glanced left and right anyway before taking my first drink.

I sat at the table and stared at the folders for a while without opening them. I put my hands on either side and positioned the bottle in front of my right hand. I nudged a folder so that it aligned with the spaces in the picnic table, those thin parallel slats between the wooden planks of the tabletop. My hands, the rectangular folders squared with the straight lines of the picnic table, the bottle uncentered in my frame of vision—*What a fine tableau*, I thought.

By the light of the fire I opened the oldest folder and began slowly looking through the statements. In most cases I couldn't remember any of it. This was years ago. What was this stuff? It felt like someone else's finances. Those first statements had credible balances, easy to pay off. It stayed that way for a while, too. Manageable expenditures followed by responsible repayments. Later, though, the balances remained. I watched it come together, the debt, as I thumbed through the statements like a flipbook. The credit limit was raised and the expenses got larger. A flight to Germany, then another to Florida, another to New York, and another. Then there was the leather furniture and a fancy racing bike. There were sums to bookstores for books I hadn't read. There were tabs at restaurants I swore I'd never eaten at. I started paging faster. At some point the spending stopped, as did the repayments. Then a plateau, the steady monotonous years of fixed amounts, the enforced repayment plan on all three cards. Which brought me to this month. I closed the folders again and let them sit on the table.

The Johnnie Walker was sharp in my mouth and seared my throat and I looked forward to running out of it. I tossed the metal cap into the fire.

I flipped the oldest folder facedown and reopened it. With the statements upside-down, I took them one at a time and turned them over. I had a last long look at the purchases and then placed them sheet by sheet into the fire. Halfway through the stack, the whisky loosened something inside of me. I started nodding at each of the statements as they went by, trying to acknowledge them. By the end, the nods were full-on bows. But I couldn't bend low enough to show them what I meant.

After about an hour, the statements were gone. Then I burned the folders. I took one last drink of Johnnie Walker and started crying, all choppy breaths and gasps for air.

After the last drink I put the empty bottle on the empty table and crawled into the mummy bag.

When I woke up, the sleeping bag was entirely soaked, but I hadn't felt a thing. I rolled up the bag and tossed it in the cab. I grabbed my book and locked the truck and headed through the willow bushes.

The beach was covered in fog. I listened for a long time to the water come in and fall over on the sand. The tide was low, so I rolled up my pants and walked out into the water all the way up to my knees. I told myself I wasn't going to get my pants wet, but sure enough, in no time I was damp up to my crotch. It was so foggy that if I closed my eyes and spun around, I couldn't tell where the shore was. I kept thinking, *I'm standing in the middle of the sea and don't know where I am.* But you know, of course, where you are, because the sea is deeper in one direction and shallower in the other. I let the clouds engulf me, though, and pretended not to have any idea.

When the fog started to evaporate, I headed toward a driftwood log and decided to read my book: Annie Dillard's *The Maytrees*. The book made a breaking sound as I sat down and opened it. Dillard stuffed so many alliterative lines into the first few pages, however, that it made me nauseous that early in the morning. There was a line about the ocean crinkling up on the shore that I liked, though, since it was happening right in front of me. *The Maytrees* goes something like this: Some people on Cape Cod court each other romantically and philosophically and fall into and out of and back into love over the course of many years. I was halfway done before the fog was gone for good. Instead of reading further, though, I decided it was time to go. I told myself that the next afternoon, when I had a break at work, I would sell it back.

On my way out of the campground I dropped the $20 bill in the registration box. The drive back was long and slow. It was Sunday, and as the cape receded behind the truck, the clouds began to dissipate. I don't know why, exactly, but the day seemed clear to me. I knew that I had just enough gas to get back to the city without refueling. I knew that in the afternoon I'd ride around the neighborhood, swooping and dipping like I do at night. As I wound my way back through the evergreens, I also knew I'd take the truck back to Tom and see what I could get for it. I tried to strategize what I might say to him, but just settled on the truth. Coming back into the city, I saw downtown and thought about Stevens'. *It's not that bad*, I thought. *And something else will come along eventually.*

Then I thought about driving back by Marie's house

to tell her how it went at the beach. But when the time came to turn, I kept going straight on toward my house. I passed the matchstick trees, watching their bare branches wave in the breeze out the truck window. Then I wondered if maybe I didn't like *The Maytrees* because I don't know anything about love. Dillard made it sound so convoluted, but I wanted love to be straightforward. Like doing basic addition instead of long division.

# 35

Another morning.

I was awakened by what seemed to be, in my drowsiness, loud crashing noises in my apartment, but it was just the cats doing feline exercises. The sun was coming in the window at a shallow angle. I got up and put on a flannel shirt, the greenish one with a missing button, and a pair of pants whose legs were still cuffed.

I turned the coffee on. As it brewed I sat and read the Sunday paper from three Sundays ago. At the back of the book section was an essay about a Saudi man who had recently purchased, book by book, an entire library to display in his home. "Everything considered classic," it said, "written in the English language." To date, the man said he had yet to read one volume. The photo of his shelves was certainly impressive.

When the coffee finished I poured a cup and took it to my closet, where I sipped it while surveying my options for the day. I've been tagging each of my items of clothing with a little note with a date and a tick for every time I've worn it. If I don't wear something in the course of this month, I'll set it on the curb—unless of course I think I can sell it, in which case I'll try that. The hot coffee felt nice in my chest. I picked out my best white shirt and decided to fish out a tie from the shoebox on the floor. For a warm outer layer, I chose my thick V-neck sweater, which sort of smelled like mustard and has a crest on it.

On the way to the kitchen I passed the mirror again. *Certainly not remarkable*, I thought, *but Jesus, it's just a fucking sink company.*

Once on the ride, I moved a little to the left in the saddle, then a little to the right, so that my bag settled comfortably on my back the way I intended when I packed it last night—long and straight items (a magazine, some pages from the paper, a notebook) at the back of the bag, and unwieldy items (carrots, wrenches, apples) building out from there, away from my body. One of the most uncomfortable situations you can have riding a bicycle is when an item with edges or round surfaces that you stashed in your bag works its way through everything else and saddles up next to your spine as you pedal. Instead of watching the road as intently as you should, you'll do anything to sneak out from beneath the sense of being stabbed from behind by an object you can't remember. You keep riding anyway, but contort every few seconds this way and that, rising up out of the saddle, then bending down, trying to lessen the vague pain. You can't for the life of you figure out what in your bag could possibly be shaped like that, not until you pull over, take everything out, lay it on the sidewalk, and finally understand what you've got.

Further on I saw two parents walking next to their two kids, pushing them on bicycles. Past that, a half dozen crows were picking at some nuts that had fallen from a tree. As I rode by, four or five of them flew up from their foraging and then along with me for a few seconds, and I took it as a good sign, this murder of crows escorting me.

Downtown, I slipped into the flow of traffic. The commuter train came up above ground, taking up a whole lane on its tracks in the street, and I rode there for several blocks alongside it. People in the compartments could see me out the window, and I them. They looked nice, and I hope they thought the same of me—my tie, my socks, my ability to ride without a coat. I wondered how warm it was in there and whether anyone was reading, about to finish a book. If so, they could take it home tonight and place it on the shelf and step back and have a look and think, *There, that one's been read.*

The train and I went along together for a spell, and then stopped at the same red light. I leaned over and rested on my handlebars. Full, billowing breaths clouded up in front of me. My socks were high and my shoes felt solidly tied, pant cuffs well away from any moving parts.

The cross street's light turned yellow. I looked down to secure my foot in the toe basket for a clean launch against the train. The conductor sounded his warning horn and I watched my foot as I placed it on the crunchy pedal. Beneath me was a traffic arrow, and my front tire rested on the tip. The arrow pointed forward up the long black street—exactly the direction I was headed.

# 36

MY WHEELS make a pleasant hum passing over wet roads. On many rides, I inadvertently go fast. I say inadvertently because I usually set out by saying to myself, "I'm going to go ahead and just take this one easy," but then something revs up in me and I see that I'm really going for it. All of a sudden I'm intentionally trying hard to be the best rider on the road. But sometimes the molecules decide to do an earnest job, and so the air is thick and the pedaling hard, as if I'm pulling the Earth behind me by a rubber band. Other days it's almost effortless.

I don't know what makes the days different, though. They just are.

# Acknowledgments

I am very grateful to the individuals who read parts of this book as it was being born and provided valuable feedback, especially Mike Burdon, Shea'la Finch, Mary Rechner, Jesse Lichtenstein, Erika Recordon, Robin Romm, Amy Gray, Lucas Bernhardt, Benjamin Craig, Melissa Reeser, and Michael Matson.

Judith Edwards, I owe you far more than this mere thanks.

Thank you also to my friend and editor Dan DeWeese, whose persistent encouragement brought this project to fruition.

## Also from Propeller Books

# *Nine Simple Patterns* for Complicated Women

STORIES • *Mary Rechner*

A woman sewing a dress for her anniversary night out finds herself presiding over her young daughters as they cut apart their own clothes. A four year old boy going earnestly about the business of being a four year old boy is perplexed as to why his behavior seems to have dramatic effects on his mother. An elementary school volunteer learns about a role-playing card game from a young boy, and then sees the roles play out in her own home.

Over the course of these nine stories, Mary Rechner brings a frank, humorous, and ultimately illuminating narrative voice to the subjects of sex, marriage, family, and work. The patient, uncompromising work of a writer who has carefully observed the moments of possibility and peril that appear—and that we often deliberately seek—in the journey from youth to adulthood, *Nine Simple Patterns for Complicated Women* is a debut collection that signals the arrival of a significant new voice in contemporary fiction.

ISBN 978-0-9827704-0-5